Reluctant Bride

Elizabeth Braden, known as Lizzie, was settling happily into spinsterhood (she claimed she never wanted to marry anyway) when two things happened. Her carriage smashed into that of Sir Edmund Blount and someone stole her diamonds.

Between Lizzie and Sir Edmund it was hate at first sight. He was an irascible tyrant and she was a spirited nag. But for reasons not even understood, Sir Edmund undertook to find Lizzie's stolen necklace – and found he was also looking for her heart.

Reluctant Bride

Joan Smith

ROBERT HALE · LONDON

ISBN 978-0-7090-7924-8

Robert Hale Limited
Clerkenwell House
Clerkenwell Green
London EC1R 0HT

www.halebooks.com

2 4 6 8 10 9 7 5 3 1

Typeset in 11½/16pt Souvenir
by Derek Doyle & Associates, Shaw Heath
Printed and bound in Great Britain
by the MPG Books Group

Reluctant Bride

CHAPTER 1

'We have done it again, Maisie – outrun the grocer.' I congratulated my aunt as we sat together in the garden trying to balance the books of Westgate Hall. 'I'll have to sell my necklace. We owe the butcher, the baker, the candlestick maker, to say nothing of the greengrocer, the modiste and the bank. Really, it is only the bank I am worried about. The mortgage comes due the end of the month. There is *no way* a hundred pounds is going to fall into our laps within a few weeks.'

'You can get an extension,' Maisie suggested, running her practiced eye over my columns of figures. She is a wizard at ciphering, but no better manager than I am myself.

'That will only delay the inevitable. And there is Jeremy's tuition to be paid in the autumn. I won't have him quit Oxford. The Braden gentlemen have always gone to Oxford. Just one more year to go; it would be a shame to pull him out.'

'It would,' she agreed sadly. Jeremy was born a scholar; read Latin and Greek as well as any university don when he was still a boy. 'On the other hand, it is not likely he will ever want to live at Westgate. He will take up teaching at the university when he graduates.'

'Yes, Aunt, and what do you and I take up? Begging? I fully intend to live out my days here, where I was born and bred. We will keep it up for Jeremy. We are close enough to the university that he can come home for holidays, even weekends if he wants.'

Westgate is not so far removed from Oxford, just a little to the northeast of Bath. It is a fine old estate, comprising five hundred acres of workable land. We have twenty tenants, mostly in dairy farming, and we have a small forest. Were it not for our tenants, we would have been in the basket long since. After my father's death, we were obliged to hire a steward, and then another to undo the disastrous work of the first. When the cure proved worse than the disease, my father's brother, Weston, came to help us out. He is nominally the guardian of the place till Jeremy reaches maturity, but an elderly scholar retired a hundred miles away in Hampshire is only a guardian on paper. He arranged the mortgage at the bank for us, and hired our third steward, Mr Berrigan, whose first clever move was to cut down half our forest before it was ready. The striplings he sent off to the lumber mill were treated as quite a joke. They were sold for kindling – fine hard-wood trees that would have brought a good price eventually, and in the interim made Westgate beautiful, instead of the way it is now, with a great gaping hole in the backdrop the forest always provided to the house.

Berrigan's next stunt was to allow some cattle disease to

run through our herd. Aphthous fever it was called. He was so busy chopping down striplings he failed to observe the cattle limping, and the blisters forming in their mouths and on their udders. Not till the milk yield was decimated and the cattle thin and lank did it occur to him there was anything amiss. By that time he had sold and traded several head, so that the disease ran rampant through our part of the country. You may imagine how popular the incident made us. We were not the only family saddled with a mortgage after the fever had done its work. Now, with no lumber to sell in the foreseeable future, and our milk yield still not up to par, we are in a fine pickle. Thank God for the tenants on the far side of the river, who managed to isolate their herds. They are all that keep us going.

'You will sell it to Weston Braden, I suppose?' Maisie asked, referring to my necklace.

'He once offered me five thousand pounds for it. I'll drop him a line and see if he is still interested. If he is not, I'll go to London and take what I can get for it there.'

'You'll not get that much. Weston's main interest in it is historical. He dotes on anything Elizabethan.'

'He most particularly dotes on my necklace. Remember, he had a copy made ten years ago when he visited Papa?'

'He says the old queen gave it to your ancestor, Sir Eldridge Braden, for helping her out of some tight political corner, but your papa had the idea she was sweet on Eldridge. There is that inscription on the silver plaque inside the box – what does it say?'

'It says, "with our extreme gratitude for your loving aid", I believe.'

'He'll want the box as well,' she warned me.

'He is welcome to it. The box is not of much value without the contents. Shall I put the ugly thing on and model it for you?'

She did not reply, but looking at my diamonds seemed a pleasant pastime after worrying over accounts for the better part of the afternoon. One ought not to have to worry about money in the last fine summer spell of the year. In August, the sun was high and hot, the greenery bereft of its first exquisite spring flush. The leaves on the trees drooped thirstily, the roses wilted on their stems. The bees droned over the thyme and stonecrop in the rockery, inducing a strange lethargy in me. I could not bother going up to my room to get my precious jewelry.

Booty, our slave of a factotum, came to us in the garden just then with a jug of lemonade. My pug, Mitzi, was at his heels, barking furiously at having been abandoned for several hours. I suddenly knew that what I wanted was not to look at the diamonds, but to draw my wicker chair into the shade and sip cold lemonade, to hold Mitzi on my lap and stroke her into silence, and daydream about what I would do when I had realized five thousand pounds for the sale of the heirloom.

Maisie, who has an uncanny way of reading my mind, drew her chair into the shadows as well, settling back with a dreamy look on her face. Maisie Belmont is an excellent companion. She talks when one wants company, is silent when one wants to dream, she does more than a lady ought to have to do around the house without a murmur of complaint, and without having any air of a drudge. She is my late mother's sister, a spinster who has lived here since my birth. She came to bear Mama company at that time, and never left. The anguish of losing my mother was greatly mitigated by having Maisie. In a way, I was closest to her, because my parents had each other, while Maisie had only me and Jeremy. She is half sister, half mother, whole friend. She has a funny, orangey color of hair, its garishness tamed now by a liberal streaking of gray. She cuts it short, as it is inclined to frizz. She has what she calls a moon face, round and pale, but enlivened with intelligent green eyes. Without ever exposing a square inch of her flesh to direct sunlight, she usually manages to have a goodly supply of freckles by summer's end. At fifty years of age, she has filled out to a roly-poly figure, which she encases in plain, dark gowns, with no pretension to fashion. Lately, the last year or so, she has suddenly begun to seem old. The fire is banking down in her spirits. The jokes are less ready, the voice taking on a querulous tone. I suppose it is the age for it – fifty. Or maybe our financial difficulties have troubled her more than she lets on. It saddens me to see her grow listless, but of course I still love her.

I glanced at her, cherishing her plain, moon face. Wouldn't it be *awful* when she was gone? Mitzi emitted one of her ugly spitting sounds as my fingers pushed too hard into her neck. I relaxed, turning purposefully to happier thoughts. I saw a halcyon future, with Jeremy established to prominence in a scholastic career, Westgate safely out of the hands of the mortgage people, a ready supply of cash invested in the funds from the sale of the necklace, Maisie and myself going cosily on in our quiet routine here at home. We are not very sociable. We take part in the local dos, of course, mostly those connected with the church and Eastgate Hall.

The estate of which our Westgate forms a corner was once annexed to Lord Beattie's domain, Eastgate. We have some slim kinship with the Beatties, going back a few centuries, but they have long since outpaced us in the accumulation of titles, wealth and prestige. Eastgate is a grander place entirely, a castle really, that resembles a stone quarry, it is built of such rough and ready material. Westgate is more refined. Our stones are shaped geometrically, and fashioned into a pretty, gothicky sort of building. Beattie once told me our place was built to house some mad relation of his, and there is actually an iron grated window in one bedroom which serves to substantiate his claim, but I do not mean to imply this bad streak runs in our blood. I am not so sure he has not a touch of it himself, but that is neither here nor there.

Lord Beattie is seventy years old, and has a son half that age. He proposed marriage to me last year – the father, I mean. He was vexed, too, when I turned him down. I felt no temptation to accept. Marriage has no attraction for me. I am one of those rare creatures who is perfectly happy without a man in her life. Other than having children, without whom the world would be a sorry place of course, I see little point in marriage. I have a home, Maisie for company, a dog to berate when I am angry and Jeremy to worry about. With all that, who needs a husband? Beattie was not my first rejection. I have not had *many* offers, but without giving the least encouragement to any gentleman, I have had a few. Churchmen seem to be attracted to me. I daresay they think I would make a fit addition to a parish. At least they would never have to fear the scandal of a wayward wife, flirting with the parishioners, wearing dashing gowns, taking too much wine or behaving in any way that would not suit them. Quite a pineapple of maidenly, modest perfection, when you come down to it. Why the womanizing Lord Beattie should have proposed remains a total mystery to me. Perhaps he is under the misapprehension that Westgate belongs to me. It does not; it is Jeremy's estate. The proposal occurred at a musical evening at his place. It was the same evening he gave me my pug dog, Mitzi.

When I had paid off Jeremy's mortgage, I would truly have earned my retirement at Westgate. I would slowly sink into a spinster like my Aunt Maisie, who is as happy as any wife you can name. Happier than most, I daresay. At least we would have no lord and master to gamble away our place, to come home roaring drunk, to curse and swear and abuse us, as I have seen many a man who is called a good husband do. But I don't mean to color myself a misogamist. I have known happy marriages – my parents', for instance. Jeremy too will make some mild lady a suitable spouse one day. He has a good disposition, and no bad habits except littering the house from end to end with open books. He flies into quite a pelter when I put them back on the shelves, which he terms 'hiding' them.

After we had finished the lemonade, and after I had

reminisced and daydreamed to my heart's content, we went indoors to change for dinner. We observe the amenities of life here at Westgate, Maisie and I. In a lighthearted mood from having taken my decision, I donned my diamonds for a final wearing before I should take them off to Uncle Weston Braden.

'Farewell performance, eh, Lizzie?' my aunt asked, with a large smile adorning her face. I made a curtsey, lifting my skirt tails to show myself off. I had worn my good green gown, to do justice to the jewels. Booty, unimpressed, hastened us toward the dining room, before our supper should grow cold.

'I decided to have a final wear out of them. I have written Weston. If he is still interested, I shall take them to him personally. It would not be safe to send them through the mail, and we cannot spare a servant. I'll drive down to Fareham myself. I may stay a week or so.'

'Do you want me to go with you?' she asked.

'That is up to you. I mean to take Mitzi along for company. At my age, I hardly require a chaperone, but if you would enjoy the trip, do come.'

'If I thought Jeremy would be coming home . . .'

'What, leave the happy halls of Oxford, when he has got the run of the library for the summer, unhampered by students? Not a chance. He has not even taken the pains to write more than once. I shan't be going for a week or five days. I must wait and hear if Weston still wants the necklace.'

'I don't think I will go. I never could care for Weston Braden. And there is that stepson of his, Glandower

Cummings, who will be grinning at us.'

'Glandower won't be there. He spends his time in London gambling and chasing heiresses. Aunt Vera complained of him in her last letter.'

'Weston is too soft with him,' she complained. 'You want to puff Jeremy off while you are there. You might pull the estate out from under that grinning Glandower yet.'

'There is no chance of it. He dotes on the boy, as he did his mother.'

'Old fool, marrying a woman half his age.'

'She was forty, Maisie. Speak no ill of the dead. It was her good fortune her son should land in the honeypot. It does Jeremy out of the Rusholme estate but then, you know, when people fall over that strange precipice called love, they lose all common sense.'

'Have *you* ever been in love, Liz?' she asked suddenly.

It was an extremely unlikely question to come from my sensible aunt. There was some strange feeling in the air that evening. A storm was brewing, causing an oppressive atmosphere, stirring dormant emotions, unsettling the soul. Streaks of lightning flashed beyond the windows, giving eerie, fleeting glimpses of black silhouettes of trees whipping wildly in the park beyond. Thunder added its ominous, angry rattle, shaking the crystal on the table, even causing the candle flames to flicker. At the far end of the room, I caught a picture of myself reflected in the mirror. It was my diamond necklace that drew my eyes to it. They danced with an orange-red-blue-purple flame. My hair looked black in reflection, though it is far from it, more of a coppery red color actually. Not orange, like Maisie's used to be.

I felt strangely as though I were looking at someone other than myself, some – *queen*. It was likely Queen Elizabeth's gift to my ancestor that called this caprice to mind. I had not realized how proudly I held my head, till that very moment. Some folks call me proud, though I do not think I am anything of the sort, you may be sure. I might accept the term assertive. I do not hesitate to speak up for my rights. At the ripe old age of twenty-five, a lady loses her girlish hesitation. I went on looking at the queen, assessing her appearance. She had rather handsome eyes, I thought. Dark and widely spaced. Her imperfect nose was concealed at the distance at which I sat from her. Her mouth looked sulky.

'Well, have you?' Maisie repeated.

'No,' I answered. 'Have you?'

'Yes, I was, once.'

'Maisie! You have been holding out on me all these years! I did not think there was much about you I did not know. Who was the lucky man?'

'Lucky he didn't get stuck with me, you mean?'

'No, lucky he earned your love.'

'Oh he didn't *earn* it. I don't think love can be earned. For myself, I never cared much for anyone who deserved me. Love is a gift, not always welcome either.'

'Was it Reverend Simms?' I asked, naming an old cleric who used to call more often than his ecclesiastical business warranted. She shook her head firmly, giving me a malevolent glare from her sharp green eyes. I named a few more gentlemen of the same kidney – dry old sticks actually.

'You have an odd idea of my taste in men!' she declared,

miffed with me.

'Who was he then? I shan't tell a soul. Promise.'

'Beattie,' she answered, with a challenging lift of her chin, as though to say, 'What of it?'

'*Lord* Beattie – *old* Lord Beattie?' I gasped.

'Not his rakeshame son. Yes, it was why I stared and then laughed like a hyena when you told me he had offered for *you*. Remember, when you told me in the carriage on the way home from the concert that he had offered, I laughed till the tears streamed down my face. In the end, I didn't know whether I was laughing or crying.'

'You are the slyest woman in the parish, Maisie Belmont! I never had a single suspicion you were sweet on him. I don't think I approve of your taste, incidentally.'

'Neither do I,' she answered quickly. 'I never did *approve* of him; I just loved him. I thought he was finally warming up to *me* that day, you see. He asked a dozen personal questions, but I realized then, when you told me, he was only quizzing to see if I would be staying here, or would expect to go with you to Eastgate. I had a wicked crush on that man twenty years ago, around the time Jeremy was born. Used to ride toward Eastgate, hoping just for a sight of him. He looked like something in those days, Liz, I can tell you.'

'But he was married at the time!'

'I know. Then when his wife died ten years later, I had another flare-up of my grand passion. I let it molder on till you told me that day he had offered for you. Laughing and making a joke of it. I wanted to strangle you – or him. Ah, well, it quenched the last of the embers for me. I gave up on him for good then.'

'Why did you decide to tell me now?' I asked. Her shoulders had slumped forward as she spoke. She looked old, not aging – *old*. It was about a year ago, when Beattie made me his ridiculous offer, that she had begun to change. If quenching the embers had done this to her, I think she would have done better to go on hoping, however futile the hope.

'I don't know why I told you,' she said, crumbling a piece of bread with her fingers, while a faraway look came into her eyes. 'You look so handsome tonight, in your diamonds, I just wondered – I mean, it is odd you never bothered to get married. Don't you ever mean to?'

'Of course not,' I said gruffly, with a last look at the queen in the mirror. Then my gaze turned back to Maisie, to see her looking just as usual – plain, settled. I found it totally incredible she should have been attracted to an outright rake and philanderer such as Beattie had been in his youth. His son was such another ne'er-do-well; he had never caused me so much as a single moment's anguish. I despised him very thoroughly. My only emotion when he married a few years ago was pity for his wife.

The storm broke as we finished our dinner. We had tea in the Rose Saloon, while the rain beat against the windowpanes, and the wind whistled down the flue. The subject of Maisie's unrequited love did not come up again. I felt she was sorry she had told me, and meant never to say another word on the subject. When I went up to my room, I removed the magic necklace, laid it with great ceremony in the green leather box with the green silk lining, bearing the little silver plaque, 'with our extreme gratitude for your loving aid.' Was it possible the queen had one of those unrequited passions for my ancestor? If so, the historians over the centuries had missed out on it. It was mentioned in no history book I ever read. I felt cheated, somehow, that I had never had even an unrequited love. A sense of urgency amounting almost to panic consumed me. Had God forgotten all about me?

When I arose next morning, all such foolish fancies were dissipated, like the storm. I was back to my normal, assertive, sensible self, giving Booty orders how to proceed during my absence, and Berrigan a good tongue-lashing to hold him in line till I returned. I would turn him off after I got back home. A few days was not sufficient time to find a good replacement.

Three days later I had an answer from Uncle Weston, claiming an interest in the diamond necklace, but stipulating that he was short of funds and could only offer thirty-five hundred. I wrote back asserting I would take four thousand, and that I would leave the next day.

'Do you come with me or not, Maisie?' I asked as I wrote the letter. 'I should tell Weston how many of us are going.'

'I might as well,' she decided. 'It will be dull here alone. There has been no word from Jeremy. I'll write him we are going, in case he planned to come home.

'We take more pains for the comfort of our menfolk than they take for ours.'

'I knew how it would be!' she flared up in Jeremy's defense. She fancies herself quite a mother to him.

'What in the world are you talking about?'

'You're mad at him because of selling your diamonds, and the poor boy doesn't even know you are doing it. You should tell him. He'd prefer to sell Westgate.'

'He couldn't care less. I'm not doing it for him, but for us. I was talking about his never writing to us.'

'How many times have you written to *him*?'

'Once, and he didn't bother to answer. You write every week. So you are coming with me, then?'

'Yes, I'll go.'

I included her name, finished up my letter and sealed it for posting. 'There, the demmed thing is done,' I said crossly.

'It is not proper for a lady to say "demmed." That is fitter talk for a guttersnipe,' she called after me as I went into the hall to place my letter on the mail tray, timing her jibe so I would be sure to hear it, but not consider it worthwhile returning to retaliate. If this fit of crankiness kept up, I would be happier without her company.

CHAPTER 2

*O*ur traveling carriage was not one of those dashing vehicles that ornament the roads of England. We did not hope to make eighty miles a day, or anything like it. As the crow flies, we are not more than eighty miles from Uncle Weston, but as the road meanders, it is more like a hundred. We would spend one night at an inn. We set upon Salisbury, a little more than half way, which would land us at Rusholme at midafternoon of the next day. We took our own old gray mare and brown bay for the first lap, not an elegant team, but they match the various hues of our carriage well enough. Its black has faded to gray, and would be brown before we had gone far, after the recent downpours we had been experiencing.

We left at a good hour in the morning, about nine, when the air was still fresh and not too warm. Maisie wore her second-best suit, saving her better outfits for the visit at Rusholme. I, the peacock, was unwise enough to wear my new jonquil muslin with a matching spencer that could be removed if the day became too warm. I had my diamonds tucked into my reticule, determined the bag would not leave my fingers till we reached our destination.

I swear we had not been on the road more than two hours, were not yet at Devizes, when it happened. The road was sparsely traveled, but some jackanapes of a fellow came roaring up at us from behind, going fifteen or sixteen miles an hour. I assumed he was one of those Corinthians whose pleasure it is to hunt the squirrel, as he was dressed like a gentleman and not a coachman. Hunting the squirrel is a pastime much indulged in by post-boys, mail drivers and other low types. The point of the game is to drive much too closely behind another carriage for half a mile or so, till the driver is vexed and angry, then suddenly surge out fast, to pass so close he brushes your wheel. Your proper hunter preys mainly on females. If he can elicit a shriek or put you into the ditch, his entertainment is complete.

Our hunter achieved both of these noble aims. Maisie and I shrieked our heads off, while John Groom drove smack into the ditch. The green bank coming up at me from the window was the last sight I saw before I was knocked out cold. When I opened my eyes some moments later, I was stretched out in an ungainly position in the ditch with a large, dark man bending over me, shaking me back to consciousness. I felt as though my skull bone had been splintered into a hundred pieces, and was rattling around inside my skin. Looking past the man's shoulder, I saw our carriage had got thrown on its side. The door must have flown open as we flipped, tossing me out by the force of it.

'Are you all right? Can you hear me?' the man asked.

I could see and hear it was a man, could distinguish vaguely a curled beaver on top of his head, and a blur of face. If only he would stop shaking my broken skull, I thought my vision might focus. I closed my eyes, trying to remember where I was, and what had happened. When I opened them, the face had assumed features. A pair of dark, worried, but mostly angry eyes stared at me intently. A great beak of a nose jutted forth beneath the eyes. There was something vaguely hawklike in the face. You know the angry look a hawk has. There were lines etched from nose to lips – full, sensuous lips that were out of place on that predatory countenance. The forehead was also etched with lines. Mitzi came whining up to me, too rattled to spit, as I am sure she felt like doing. I know I did.

'Cracker, go for a sawbones. She's bleeding,' the man called over his shoulder, then reached down and brushed my hair from my temple. When his fingers came away, they were smeared with my blood. It was sufficient to send me off into another bout of vapors. I am annihilated by the sight of blood, especially my own.

The next time I got my eyes and ears open, the man had discovered there was more than one passenger in our carriage and was in the process of lifting Maisie out the door. She hung like a rag doll in his arms. I struggled to my feet, staggered to the closest tree, till the ground ceased rotating beneath me, turned from black and blue to green, then I went falteringly toward them. Mitzi dragged along behind me. I was petrified to see poor Maisie looking entirely lifeless.

'You've *killed* her!' I said, in a whisper.

'Rubbish! She's unconscious,' the man answered roughly, though he looked extremely worried. He placed her on the ground. 'Watch her,' he ordered me, as he jumped up and ran to the road.

There was a frisky gig coming toward us, pulled by a single nag. He hailed it, and another gentleman hopped down to offer his aid. The newcomer had the air of a bumptious squire. You can spot them a mile away, with their self-important manner, their provincial accents and their poor tailoring.

'These women are hurt. Are you from around here? Where can I take them to be seen to?' our accident-prone friend asked, in the most overbearing way imaginable, as though the whole affair were a great imposition on his time and patience.

'My own place is just two miles down the road. I would be happy to help,' the squire offered.

'Two miles? Christ, they'll have bled to death before they are taken half that distance. Is there nowhere closer? An inn, a farm house. . . .' He looked around as he spoke, but there was no building in sight.

'Devizes is only half a mile yonder,' the squire told him.

'Help me get them into my rig, will you?' he asked, but in an imperative tone. 'The younger one is conscious. She can walk to it. The old lady will have to be hauled.'

I was kneeling over Maisie, chaffing her hands, trying to rouse her, while this genteel conversation went forth. 'Hauled' as if she were a load of rubbish. The two men came forward, elbowing me aside to lift Maisie from the ground. The squirrel hunter's carriage was not in the ditch, but resting on the shoulder of the road. They were about to place Maisie on a banquette, when suddenly the carriage leaned sharply to the left. A wheel had been broken, but had not fallen till the weight was placed on it. An accomplished curse rent the air. I am happy to say Mitzi had recovered, and took offense at the offender. She has no great love for men. She behaves well with females, but will often take to spitting at loud gentlemen. I usually try to curb her, but let her hiss away on this occasion.

'We'll have to use your rig,' the dark man told the squire. 'We won't all be able to fit in it. You take the ladies to Devizes. I'll stay here and send the doctor on to the inn when he comes, if he comes. I've sent a boy off for him.'

The squire agreed. 'I'll take them to the Rose and Thistle, if you think my rig can hold three of us.'

'Of course it can. The girl will have to hold the old lady. Miss,' he said, glancing toward me.

I was still too dazed to object to his arrogant manner, and too worried for Maisie's life. I was helped into the gig, Maisie was lifted up to be propped between the squire and myself. She was beginning to return to consciousness.

'Lizzie, you're hurt!' was her first speech. The blood from my temple was trickling down the side of my face. The man, not the squire, handed me a handkerchief, which I took without a word and held against my aching temple.

'You'll need your hands,' he said. He undid my bonnet ribbons to tie his handkerchief around my head, like a pirate's kerchief. As soon as he was done, I untied it and gave it back to him, blood and all.

'Hand up my dog,' I said. Mitzi was wagging her tail at the gig's wheels, beginning to make those sounds which she thinks are barks, though they aren't really.

He shoved her from him, not kicking her exactly, but just nudging her away. 'There's no room. I'll bring the mutt along with me.' Mitzi hissed and spit angrily. I fully expected she would get a kick or cuff before she joined me, but really I was not able to handle her in my condition.

Just as he gave the squire the signal to go forward, Maisie said, 'The necklace, Lizzie. . . .'

Till that instant, I had forgotten my diamonds completely. I felt such a spasm of fear for their safety! 'Oh, my reticule!' I exclaimed.

'I'll bring it to the inn,' the man assured me.

'No, I must have it now.'

'I don't see it,' he said, after one brief glance to the road-way at his feet.

'Maybe it is still in our carriage. I *must* have it.'

With a grunt of aggravation he lumbered off to our carriage, clambered in and came out with Maisie's black patent reticule. Mine was a summer bag, of yellow kid. I sent him off to look again. It was not in the carriage. 'Go along. I'll find it,' he said.

When I propped Maisie against the squire and began to climb down, he went for a more thorough search. It eventually turned up a dozen feet from that spot where I first regained consciousness, in the ditch. It was hanging open when he gave it to me. He hadn't the sense to snap it shut. I looked inside to see the green leather jewelry case was safely within. Maisie had recovered sufficiently to ask me if everything was all right, which mysterious statement meant were the diamonds safe. I told her everything was fine, and we were off.

The squire was very helpful. His self-consequence earned respect at the Rose and Thistle. He was called Squire Bingeman, indicating he was well-known locally. He helped me get Maisie settled on a sofa, ordered wine, hot water, basilicum powder and bandages, in readiness for the doctor's arrival. I had the feeling he was relishing the exciting interlude in his daily life, or relishing the excuse to order servants about in any case. He issued his commands with a certain satisfaction. They were promptly obeyed. When he had us settled, he went into the lobby, ostensibly to look out for the doctor, but when there was no sign of him, he said he would just take a stroll into the tavern, where I imagine he was expounding to the customers his role as good samaritan.

He was not gone a minute before Maisie suddenly went off in another faint, her face as pale as paper. I darted into the hall for help. There was a gentleman just passing the door. Seeing my state of distraction, he sprang forward to offer his assistance. He was a handsome fellow, tall and fair, outfitted in the first style of elegance.

'Is there something wrong, ma'am? Can I do anything for you?' he asked.

'My aunt – she's fainted,' I replied, quite at random, wondering in what way he could help.

The clerk came forward and explained the situation, giving him my name while he was about it, though he did not tell me who the gentleman might be.

'Let us see what can be done,' he offered at once, following me into the parlor.

He was thoroughly capable. For a moment I thought I had had the good fortune to have bumped into a doctor. He flung open the window to give her fresh air, chaffed her hands, ordered me to pull the feather from her bonnet for burning – all the while assuring me in a calming way that her plight was not serious. The color was seeping back into her cheeks. He drew out his watch to time her pulse. After she had rallied somewhat, I said to him, 'Are you a doctor, sir?'

He laughed, showing a set of flashing white teeth. 'Indeed, no, though I would like to have been one. My family felt it beneath me. I am an army man, Colonel Fortescue, at your command, ma'am.'

'A colonel!' I exclaimed, smiling my delight at his high position.

'Retired – sent home from the Peninsula for a wound in the chest. A scratch merely. The doctors feared for my lungs, but I swear the bullet was nowhere near them. Just here under the left arm it caught me,' he outlined. He made little of it, but I noticed a spontaneous wince of pain seized his features when he clutched too hard at his wound.

'You have been very kind, Colonel. Everyone has been extraordinarily kind. Thank you so much.'

'It is always a pleasure to have the honor of helping a lady in distress. Dare I inquire, a *damsel* in distress?' he inquired archly.

'Yes,' I answered.

'I thought the clerk said *Miss* Braden. Are you from around here, ma'am?'

'We live a few miles north, at Westgate. We are going to Fareham.'

'Pity, I hoped you might say you were *en route* to London, as I am myself, so that I would have the pleasure of calling on you. Fate is perverse, is she not? Just when you meet someone. . . .' He came to a flustered halt, smiled rather shyly. 'You must forgive these Spanish manners I contracted in the Peninsula. We officers have to rush our few chance acquaintances with the ladies.'

He seized my fingers to make his *adieux*. I was struck most forcibly by a wish that it had been this charming colonel who had run us off the road, and not the hawklike man. He had the nicest eyes, dark blue, with lashes a yard long. The eyes were tinged with regret at the necessity to leave. He was not gone long before Bingeman returned to pester us.

I had a glass of the wine he had ordered. It helped me regain my spirits, but augmented my headache. I felt extremely nervous and quite weak. A peep into the mirror told me I also looked a fright. It was a wonder the colonel had bothered to inquire my name. Till the doctor came, there was nothing to do but sit and wait and worry. Maisie was beginning to complain of a wrenched ankle, which was indeed swollen when I lifted her skirt to take a look. The squire was at my elbow, eager for a glimpse. He also put his hand on my shoulder in a way I did not like, though I hesitated to call him to account after his kindness. When the hand slid in a seemingly careless way to my waist, however, I found it possible to lift it away, without any verbal rebuke.

Within a quarter of an hour, the doctor arrived with the man who had caused all our difficulties. We were exciting a good deal of curiosity at the inn. Every servant and half the patrons came to the door on some pretext or other – offering help or just plain inquiring what had happened. Several of them got right inside. I shooed them out and bolted the door.

'Make it snappy,' the squirrel hunter ordered the doctor. 'I am in a hurry. I'm very late for my appointment already. Just let me know the ladies are in no danger and I'll be on my way. Naturally, I shall settle for all expenses.'

'If you and Squire Bingeman would care to step outside, Sir Edmund, I will examine the older lady first. She seems to be in the worse case,' the doctor replied.

I now had a name for our malefactor. 'Our carriage must also be repaired, Sir Edmund,' I said, eager to get it arranged before he darted off on us.

'Naturally. I said I would stand buff,' he answered, offended. Then he turned to the squire. 'You are a local fellow, Bingeman. Would you take care of having the ladies' carriage and horses tended to for me? Tell them to charge it to Sir Edmund Blount. Maybe I ought to leave some money. They may not know me here. I'm from Gloucester.'

'You'll be leaving your own carriage and horses as well, Sir Edmund,' the squire pointed out. 'They'll not be wanting more collateral than those bits of blood. I think one of

your nags has got a nasty sprain in her left foreleg. I would-
n't take them on the road after the spill. Nags are easily
excitable.'

'That's true. My groom will take care of my rig, but he
only has two hands. Will you see to theirs?'

'The inn will send a lad down the road to do it,' the
squire answered.

Sir Edmund cast a defeated, angry glance at the man
and went out the door. He had met someone as unbidda-
ble as he was himself. Bingeman went out behind him. The
doctor spent about twenty minutes in his ministrations to
Maisie. Her ankle was deemed to be sprained, not broken.
He bound it up tightly and suggested she stay off it for a
few days, then he turned to me. Both Bingeman and
Blount felt free to return once Maisie's skirt was pulled
back down. My little scratch was washed and had a plaster
stuck on it.

'That doesn't need anything. It's only a scratch,' Blount
told the doctor.

I immediately revised my plan of removing the plaster
the instant the doctor left. 'She'll live,' the doctor agreed.
'Anything else hurt?' he asked, running an eye over my
body.

'My back is wrenched quite painfully. Will it be possible
for us to continue on with our trip, Doctor, if my aunt stays
off her ankle? Just hobble from the inn to a carriage is all
that she will have to do.'

'It would be better to rest for a day first. Especially with
a sore back.'

'Your carriage certainly won't be fixed today,' Sir

Edmund reminded me.

'You are not the only one who has urgent business, sir! It happens *we* are also in a hurry,' I answered sharply.

'There is no mad panic to get to Rusholme,' Maisie said. I glared at her. 'Where are they, Lizzie? Are they safe?' she asked in a low voice, referring to the diamonds, which kept slipping from my mind with all the other matters weighing on it. I looked around for my reticule, to see it sitting on a chair precariously close to the door. There was hardly a soul at the inn who had not been at that door within the past half hour too. I snatched it up quickly and held on to it.

'You'd better let *me* watch it, as your wits are gone begging,' she said, taking the reticule from me.

'It happens I have some business to tend to myself,' Bingeman said, beginning to make his bows. We expressed our thanks and appreciation, he expressed his consolation and good wishes, and finally he left. The doctor was prevailed upon by Sir Edmund and myself to find Maisie and me fit to travel, and he too left, after some money changed hands at the door.

'As I mentioned, I am in a hurry,' Sir Edmund said, turning back to us. 'I shall settle the bill here, and arrange a hired carriage and team for you at the stable where I am going to get one for myself. I don't know what your business may be, but *I* am on my way to a wedding, which takes place in an hour, more than fifteen miles away. I shall leave you my card with my name and address, in case any additional expense should arise as a result of this mishap.' He reached into his pocket for a card as he spoke. 'I am sorry for the wretched bother I have caused you. I have one suggestion to make, ladies.'

I looked with some interest to hear what he might have to say. 'Hire a coachman who knows how to drive. That Johnnie Trot will land you in another accident. I never saw such a cow-handed fellow.'

I stood with my mouth opening and closing silently. I was beyond speech for thirty seconds. 'Well upon my word!' I said when speech returned. 'If this doesn't beat all the rest! *You* run us into the ditch, sprain our team, destroy our carriage, nearly kill the pair of us and suggest *we* find a new coachman! I suggest *you* find a new road, build yourself a private one, if you insist on driving like a mad fiend.'

'I happen to be an excellent sawyer, ma'am. I have been driving upwards of fifteen years and have never had an accident before. Your man veered towards me as I cut out to pass, as greenhorns will often do.'

'Then you should have been ready for it, if it *often* happens!'

'I was, but my team, unfortunately, is new and city-bred, so such country driving as they encountered today found them unprepared.'

I took a deep breath to give him a piece of my mind. The words were never uttered. It was Maisie who spoke. 'Lizzie, they're *gone!*' she wailed, sounding much as one imagines an Irish banshee would sound.

'What are you talking about?' I asked, turning to look at her. She held the green leather jewel case in her fingers. She was turning it upside down, shaking it, as though a large diamond necklace had become lost in a perfectly flat sheet of silk.

'They must have fallen into my reticule,' I said, stepping forward to pull the bag from her shaking fingers.

I do not keep a neat reticule. It was stuffed to overflowing with money bag, handkerchief, comb, powder box, hartshorn, pins, needles, thread, pencil and paper – the usual necessities of a lady traveler. I rooted through the mess, becoming wild with panic as I felt my way deeper and deeper into the depths.

'What is missing?' Blount asked, smiling hatefully at my rummaging.

'My diamonds.'

He pulled the reticule from my hands, walked to the table and dumped the whole contents into a heap, to rifle through them. Then, like Maisie with the green box, he shook the empty purse, to see if the diamonds fell out of nowhere. 'Sure you put them in here?' he asked.

'Yes. Are *you* sure they have not found their way into *your* pockets?' I asked, in a voice every bit as rude as his own.

There was a stunned silence. Even *I* was shocked I had had the gall to utter my first suspicion. 'I beg your pardon!' Sir Edmund asked in a high, incredulous tone.

'Do you, Sir Edmund? It is the first time today it has occurred to you to beg our pardon for all the bother you have caused us!' Once it was out, you know, I could not very well back down, so meant to brazen it through.

'I will not be accused of this!' he said, his eyes wide open, shooting sparks, while his full lips pulled into a thin line, white around the edges. 'Do you know who you are talking to?'

'I don't care a groat who you are. You *are* accused, sir.'

'No, really, Lizzie,' Maisie cautioned, twitching at the skirt of my gown, as she used to do twenty years ago when I misbehaved.

'What do we know about him?' I asked her, making no effort to hide my words. 'We don't know a thing about this man but that he *calls* himself Sir Edmund something or other, and is a very bad driver. I can call myself Queen Charlotte, but it does not make me her. How do we know he means to pay for our carriage either, or hire us another at the stable? He can walk out of here with my diamonds in his pockets and we may never see him again.'

Sir Edmund's mouth fell open in shock. He stared, literally beyond words. 'Well, sir, may we see your pockets emptied?' I asked boldly.

'No, madame, you may not!'

'You see, he's got them!' I crowed triumphantly.

Sir Edmund glared for about sixty seconds in dead silence, breathing rapidly, while on his face I read the determination not to satisfy me argue with his desire to prove his innocence. At length, he began slowly, one pocket at a time, to pull the linings out for inspection. First the jacket, unbuttoned and the inner pockets turned out. They contained a spare handkerchief, a black leather money purse and a few personal cards. Then the trousers, which contained a ring of keys, a small black comb, a miniature pearl-handled pen knife, a fish hook, some loose change and a piece of paper with a girl's name and

address scribbled on it. He said not a word throughout the
ceremony, but only glared as if he would like to shoot me.
When he had finished, he said, 'Would you like me to
remove my clothing and boots as well, Miss Braden?' On
that sarcastic speech, he did actually remove his jacket,
shook it, ran his hands over his shirt, which revealed no
suspicious bulges. 'Satisfied?' he asked, 'or shall I take off
the trousers?'

I waited a moment before speaking, as though I were
considering this point. I picked up one of his cards in a
careful way to assure myself he had been calling himself Sir
Edmund Blount long enough to have cards made up in the
name at least. He was from Woldwood, in Gloucester. The
name and place had a vaguely familiar sound to me. I
thought some of our tainted cattle had found its way that
far north, where they were very ill received. When I
glanced up, he was still glaring.

'I expect an apology. If you were a gentleman, I would
call you out,' he said in cold, measured accents.

'If I was wrong, I am sorry,' I said, with no hesitation.

'You *were* wrong.'

'I am not wrong that my diamonds are gone. They were
in that green case when I left home this morning. If not
you, then someone else . . .' Already my mind was flying
back over the morning, with several unfortunate lapses
during which I had been unconscious. 'If you didn't take
them, it is certainly your fault they are gone,' I pointed out,
with some justification I think. 'It happened some time
after the accident.'

'Your reticule was open when I found it in the ditch.

That must be when they fell out.'

'The box was closed when we left the accident. At least – yes, I'm sure it was.'

'It's worth a look, back down the road. How valuable is it?'

'Five thousand pounds.'

'Why the devil were you carrying it around the country-side loose and unprotected?' he asked, beginning to stuff his contents back into his pockets.

'I had not planned on being dumped unconscious in a ditch, Sir Edmund, or put on public display in a second-rate inn, with an underbred squire mauling me.'

'Lizzie! Was he indeed?' Maisie asked, horrified.

'He was trying to.'

'I didn't like the cut of him above half. A very disobliging fellow. Wouldn't even go to the stable for me,' Blount added.

'He was suddenly in a great hurry to leave, too!' Maisie remembered.

'It could have been the doctor,' I said.

'Or that smiling colonel who was in here, rolling his eyes at you,' Maisie pointed out.

'He was not rolling his eyes! He was very nice. It could have been any one of the servants,' I said, beginning to realize my task was impossible, with such a surfeit of suspects.

'Bingeman had more chance than any of them,' Blount pointed out. 'He was here, and he was at the accident. I am going to pay him a call.'

'You cannot accuse him outright of theft!' I said.

'You accused *me*! Ladies do not understand these matters. My honor is at stake. Well, I must accept *some* responsibility for the loss, though I still cannot comprehend why you were carrying them around loose in your reticule. If I hurry, I might catch him before he leaves the inn.' He was already hastening to the door as he spoke, his long legs flashing.

'He said he had some business . . .' Maisie said.

Bingeman's voice, notwithstanding his business, was heard in the hallway at that moment. He was taking his leave of the proprietor. It occurred to me he would not have tarried so long if he had a stolen necklace in his pocket. He had been treated with respect at the inn, too – was obviously a gentleman of character. This did not occur to Blount, who bolted to the door and asked him to step into our parlor. It was an extremely embarrassing interlude. I knew as soon as Blount spoke that the man was innocent.

'Miss Braden finds a valuable diamond necklace is missing from her reticule,' he said, in a meaningful way.

Bingeman did not misunderstand him. Not a word of commiseration did the squire utter. 'I hope you are not implying *I* had anything to do with the loss,' he answered hotly.

'I am very much afraid we will have to ask you to prove it,' Blount replied in an odiously toplofty way.

In lieu of proving it, Bingeman let fly his right fist, which caught Blount on the chin and lifted his toes from the floor. Less than a second elapsed before the blow was returned. Within another second, the proprietor was at the door, trying to bring peace, but as our combatants were at it hammer and tong by this time, the owner took the misguided notion of sending off for a constable instead. My dog, whom I had heard yelping in the hallway for some few minutes, finally found me. She came rocketing through the doorway to add her noisy presence to the scene. When the Law arrived, Bingeman was flat on the floor having his pockets rifled by Blount. Mitzi was the only one trying to prevent him. She had attached her sharp little teeth to his boot. Being caught in such an illegal act, Blount was promptly hauled off to the roundhouse by the local constable.

Bingeman went along to press charges, intimating over his shoulder that if the story of diamonds was more than a story, *he* would be much surprised. Mitzi took a leap at his knees for good measure, but was swotted off by the squire. I gathered her up in my arms to keep her from further mischief, vowing to myself I would not be so foolhardy as to venture upon another trip with a dog.

'Congratulations! You've really done it *this* time, Lizzie,' Maisie said. She was trying to pretend she was angry, but in truth the excitement of our day had brought a glow to her eyes.

'It's not my fault. Who thought Blount would be so stupid as to accuse him with no proof? We've got to get him out, Maisie.'

'Let him stay in jail. We're well rid of the troublesome fellow, which is *not* to say your behavior has been anything but outrageous!'

'We are not well rid of his money. Blount is to pay the

bill here, repair our carriage, meanwhile hire us a new one. I haven't enough cash to do it. No, we have got to get him out.'

' 'Twas Bingeman that struck the first blow,' Maisie remembered.

'So it was. Blount ought to be laying charges himself. Assault.'

'Except that he slandered Bingeman first. That could be a serious matter.'

'It will all end up in *my* dish. *I* first slandered Blount, though you are the only one who heard me. It was not public at all.'

'I wish they'd put that mutt of yours behind bars till we get back. What possessed you to drag that spitter along?'

'It's not Mitzi's fault,' I said, patting her head – the dog's, I mean. 'Good Mitzi.'

'What a disgusting display! You talking babytalk to a *dog*. You never showed half so much affection to your brother or your father, or mother for that matter, as you lavish on that mutt. You're turning senile, Lizzie.' She jiggled angrily around on the sofa for a few minutes before continuing with her rant. 'I cannot go trailing down the street with this ankle. It hurts like the devil.'

'I'll go alone. I look a perfect witch, or a lady bruiser with this patch on my forehead. God knows what credence will be placed on my testimony. I'll be lucky if I don't end up in the roundhouse myself. I had better leave Mitzi with you. I don't want her biting the constable. If I don't come back. . . .'

'If you don't come back, I'm not going after you. Not

one step. I'll hire a nag and go home. Should we let Jeremy know?'

'For what purpose? It would make a very dull subject for a Grecian ode.'

'Run along then. And Liz. . . .'

I mistrusted the forlorn sound of the last speech. 'What is it?'

'We still haven't found the diamonds,' she reminded me. It is really astonishing how many times that day I managed to forget the reason for undertaking the journey in the first place. They had slipped my mind again, completely.

CHAPTER 3

*O*fficer Peoples was the person with whom I had to contend at the roundhouse. I am happy to say Squire Bingeman had departed after having given his testimony. I saw him leave in his gig as I entered the door. Officer Peoples was a nervous tic who more closely resembled a skeleton than a man: he was skin and bones. He appeared to hold the squire in high esteem, almost in fear. Sir Edmund was in the process of having a pair of manacles attached to his wrists when I barged in unceremoniously. I do not think the constable had much chance of accomplishing the task he had in mind. Blount looked ready to strike him to the ground. He did not look one jot happier when I came in, either.

'Is this here the woman you was talking about? Her that had her alleged diamonds stoled?' Peoples asked, surveying me with lively interest. He had perfectly round, little blue eyes, as blue as the sky on a summer's day.

'There has been a wretched mistake here, Officer,' I said, assuming an air of injured nobility. Blount looked interested, no more.

'Aye, so there has, Miss. But we'll catch un, never fear.'

'This is not the man who stole the necklace,' I pointed out.

'The *alleged* necklace,' Peoples corrected, with a knowing blue eye trained sharply on me. 'Maybe this is your thief and maybe it ain't. What I'm booking un for is infamous slander and assault. The squire is a big man, hereabouts. A body don't go slandering the squire if he knows what's good for him. Why, he sits down to drink an ale with Lord Purdy twice a week, and has his own Member run up to Parliament. Now, sir, I'll have your alleged name,' he demanded, turning to Blount.

With a wary face, Blount answered, 'Edmunds.'

'Mr Edmunds,' the constable said, nodding his head.

'*Sir* Edmund!' I corrected hastily, rather wishing I had made it Lord Edmund instead, as the constable appeared to dote on a title. 'And you are not booking Sir Edmund for anything. A mistake occurred. *I* told Sir Edmund that the squire took my diamonds.'

'Alleged diamonds,' he pointed out, but the 'Sir' was getting to him. The manacles had found their way to his desk, and were being hastily shuffled under a stack of papers.

'If you mean to lock anyone up in those disgusting contraptions, it must be me. Sir Edmund was no more than an innocent bystander,' I said.

'Ha! Innocent is it, Miss? The squire tole me hisself this

here fellow landed him a facer.'

'Self-defense!' I said firmly. 'I witnessed the whole. Bingeman landed the first blow. If you mean to charge Sir Edmund Blount with anything, I shall personally lay a charge against Squire Bingeman.' Just what charge I could possibly lay was not clear yet, but I would dredge up something. Molesting was a possibility.

I became aware, as I spoke, that Sir Edmund was displeased with my performance. A black scowl had settled on his countenance. He stood behind the constable, shaking his head negatively, and giving other mute indications that he wished me to desist. I could not make heads or tails of it. Was it possible he *wanted* to be locked up?

I believe the idea of charging Bingeman with something appealed to Peoples. It was not hard to credit the squire had made himself obnoxious. 'What is you charging un with, then, the squire?' he asked, smiling to reveal a few chipped remains of teeth.

'Assault with intent to cause bodily harm. He struck the first blow. I witnessed it. My aunt, Lady Braden, witnessed it. We are ready to testify,' I said grandly, having given Maisie a title to impress the constable.

'*Sir* Edmund, did ye say?' Peoples confirmed.

'That is correct. Sir Edmund Blount, from Woldwood in Gloucester. You would be familiar with the name of course.'

'Oh, aye!' he said, vastly impressed. The blue eyes were all but popping. 'But how do I know he's him?'

'Show him one of your cards, Sir Edmund,' I suggested.

Sir Edmund scowled again. He reluctantly drew out one of his cards. The constable took it, waved it a few moments in his fingers, like a fan, stuck it between his front teeth, chewed on it, then took his decision. 'Lady Braden was your aunt's name, you said?' he asked.

'That is correct. The Countess of Braden, lady in waiting to Her Majesty, Queen Charlotte. Gracious, I *do* hope it will not be necessary to pester Her Majesty with this trifling business. If the Prince must be disturbed over this picayune affair, he will be out-of-reason cross,' I said, bombarding him with every great title I could lay tongue to.

'Oh, well, we won't be disturbing Her Majesty,' the constable decided. Next he was struck down with a fit of chivalry. He bowed to me, very ceremoniously, nearly scraping the floor with his nose. When he came up, he said, 'And ye would be willing to swear, if it came to court, that the squire landed the first blow.'

'Categorically.'

'Categorically,' he repeated, memorizing the word. He scratched the side of his head, considered for an important amount of time, jotted the word 'categorically' down on a piece of paper and finally decreed. 'I'll let Sir Edmund go then, in your custody, Lady Braden.'

'Lady Braden?' I asked, raising my brows imperiously. 'You are extremely ignorant, my good man. My *aunt* is Lady Braden. I am Lady Elizabeth.'

'That's what I meant!' he said quickly, performing another bow.

'Come along, Sir Edmund,' I urged. 'Be a good fellow,

do, and don't lay a charge against that odious upstart squire.'

The constable smiled invitingly. 'It could be done with no trouble a-tall,' he volunteered.

Blount never showed a single trace of a smile through-out my performance. 'It is up to you, Lady Elizabeth,' he said in a thin voice.

'We'll let him off with it *this* time. If his manners do not improve, however, we may reconsider the matter.'

'About your alleged diamonds, your ladyship,' Peoples said. 'That is – your diamonds.'

'Are you quite sure you did not loan them to Princess Marie again, Lady Elizabeth?' Blount inquired.

'Perhaps I did. I'll ask her as soon as we get to London.' I picked up Blount's curled beaver from the desk, handed it to him, gave a curt nod to the constable and got out the door as fast as I could, while maintaining a noble quantity of dignity.

I was trembling when we got to the street. 'Lady Elizabeth, eh?' was Blount's first comment.

'I borrowed the title to impress that toadeater. Why were you frowning behind his back? He would have let you out in a trice if you had pulled rank on him.'

'I was not eager to have my name appear on a public record for assault and battery. Mr Edmunds meant to pay a fine and leave.'

'You are inordinately proud of the name. You would have had your carcass behind bars if you had remained Mr Edmunds.'

He placed his curled beaver on his head, brushed off his

jacket with the back of his hands, lifted his chin to indicate I was to tag along and struck out at a long stride for the inn. 'Any word on the alleged diamonds during my absence?' he asked.

'I left a few minutes after you. I haven't heard anything.'

'You certainly placed me in an extremely embrrassing position, indicating Bingeman was a thief,' was his next cheerful speech.

'Sir Edmund, you know *perfectly well you* were the one who jumped to that conclusion!'

'Who else could it possibly have been?' he asked, in lieu of answering my charge.

'Anyone. Half the inn staff and customers poked their heads and bodies into that so-called private parlor. It could have been anyone.'

'Your aunt mentioned a colonel. I believe he did more than poke his head in at the door. There was talk of rolling his eyes at you.'

'*He* is the only *decent* soul I met. Colonel Fortescue – he was extremely helpful when Miss Belmont took a fainting spell. A veteran, wounded in the Peninsula. Certainly he had nothing to do with it. He would hardly have given me his name and destination, and expressed a hope to see me again. . . .'

'I see it was not robbery he had in his mind, but flirtation.'

'I'll never find my diamonds.'

'You don't mean to give up?' he asked, coming to a dead halt in the middle of the street.

'No, of course not. I'll have the proprietor search the

inn. Oh, but I know it is useless. There has been so much time to get rid of them, hide them I mean, whoever took them.'

'How would anyone have known you carried them?' he asked, in a puzzled way.

'I don't suppose the thief *did* know. He probably snatched up my reticule looking for money, but when he saw a jewelry case, he opened it and took the jewelry instead. My money was not stolen.'

'A regular pickpocket would have taken both.'

'He didn't have much time, and there were a lot of people standing or milling about.'

'A stupid thing to do, carry diamonds in your reticule. We'll go to the inn, quiz the proprietor. If nothing turns up there, I'll go back to where we collided and have a close search of the area where I found your reticule. They might have fallen to the ground.'

'That is kind of you, but you are in a hurry. You mentioned you were going to a wedding.'

'That is not important.'

'Who is getting married?'

'My young brother.'

'Your brother! You will not want to miss that!'

'He didn't expect me to attend. He knew I was against the match. I only decided at the last minute to go, which is why I was driving a little more recklessly than usual. They won't delay the ceremony on my account.'

'Why were you against the match?' I asked, my interest rising. 'Is there something amiss with the girl?'

'No, she is unexceptionable. Young, pretty, an heiress, well-born.'

'Why are you against it then?' I asked.

'On general principles. I disapprove of marriage. Besides, poor Willie is too young.'

I envisaged a teenaged groom, and understood at last why he was averse to the wedding. 'How old is Willie?'

'Twenty-seven.'

'Twenty-seven?' I asked, my surprise showing in my voice. 'How old must he be, before you consider him mature enough to make up his mind?'

'When he is old enough to decide *against* marriage, then he has reached the age of reason,' my companion answered firmly.

I could think of no sensible reply to such a piece of foolishness.

'Did anyone know you were traveling with the necklace?' he asked in a sudden change of subject.

'No. Only my uncle from Fareham. Certainly he had nothing to do with it.'

'You are on your way to visit him?'

'Yes.'

'An accidental discovery and theft, then, as you mentioned. That will be difficult to trace.'

'I don't expect you to waste your time helping me.'

'I don't intend to. *Waste* my time, I mean. The accident is my fault, in part. My character has become involved willy-nilly. I must assist you. I have nothing better to do in any case, as I have missed poor Willie's wedding.'

'You could be there in time for the party, even if you

missed the ceremony.'

'Would you prefer I *not* assist you? You will pardon my speaking quite frankly, Miss Braden, but from what I have seen of you and your aunt, I do not think your chances of recovering it without any assistance to be very great. In fact, they are negligible.'

'What does that mean?'

'You have not an iota of sense between the pair of you. You carry a valuable set of diamonds loose in a reticule; you accuse me with no reason whatsoever of having stolen them; you go pelting down to the roundhouse spouting nonsense of queens and princes. . . .'

'I got you out, didn't I?'

'It chanced the constable was unduly impressed with bad acting. Had he been a different sort of man and challenged your statements, you would have been revealed as a liar. Who would have believed your tale of missing diamonds after that?'

'*Alleged* diamonds,' I reminded him. 'But really, you know, my business at the roundhouse had nothing to do with the theft. It was your slander and assault of Bingeman that took me. The alleged diamonds are irrelevant.'

'It is an interesting thing, you know, so far as I am concerned, the diamonds are only an allegation. *I* have not seen them.'

'You have seen the box! I would not carry an empty box around with me in my reticule.'

'Why not? You carry everything else, to say nothing of traveling with that pugnacious pug. But this is pointless bickering,' he said, making an effort to control his vile temper. 'We shall go to the inn to see how your aunt goes on, then proceed as I mentioned earlier.'

We did just that, all of it at top speed. There is something about a bad-tempered person that causes him to act quickly. Sir Edmund walked, talked and acted very fast. I had time to catch my breath at one point. After he had thoroughly quizzed the innkeeper, who had done some quizzing and searching himself during our absence, he was convinced the man knew nothing. Sir Edmund then hired a carriage and team and returned to the scene of the accident to search the ditch and environs. Maisie and I had a cup of tea while he was gone, and I rested. Before long he was back, still going at top speed. The proprietor came into the parlor behind him, shaking his grizzled head.

'Bad publicity for me,' he said. 'First a gold watch, then a diamond necklace. Folks will be afraid to come to me.'

The three of us turned on him as one to demand an explanation for the gold watch. 'Why, this very same morning a customer of mine had a gold watch lifted from his pocket. It happened while the excitement of the accident was going forth, we figured,' he told us. 'I made sure you knew. Everyone was talking about it, but the one lady was here alone in the parlor, and you two were – out. That is how it comes you didn't hear. The victim figures he's got a line on the fellow who did it. Another customer thought the lad in the green jacket was acting odd-like, bumping into folks and taking his time about disengaging himself.'

'You mean to tell us you had a pickpocket at the inn, and didn't bother to tell us till now!' Sir Edmund howled, nonplussed.

'I was sure you knew.'

'I know who you mean!' Maisie declared, starting up from the sofa, but soon returning to her seat. 'The green jacket – I saw the fellow right here in this room. I noticed him in particular, a funny, rolling eye he had in his head, wall-eyed, like Blossom, Lizzie.' Blossom is one of our milchers, who is afflicted with a rolling eye.

'That's the one,' the proprietor told her.

'Who was the other victim?' Blount asked.

'His name was Colonel Fortescue. A very nice-seeming gentleman. He stopped off last night, was waiting to meet someone, but his party did not arrive. He's been watching the roads all morning. I believe it was his sister who was to come.'

'Oh, the colonel, Maisie!' I exclaimed. 'What a pity. Imagine robbing a wounded veteran.'

More to the point, Blount said, 'You mentioned someone had a line on the fellow. Where did he go?'

'He straddled a rattler to Winchester,' the owner answered readily. 'Colonel Fortescue was told the lad was seen running toward the coaching office. He went after him and learned he bought a ticket to Winchester. He came back and told me of the lad's destination, in case anyone else discovered a watch or money missing.'

'Why the devil didn't you tell us this hours ago?' Blount demanded.

'I didn't know the pickpocket was in this parlor! How

should I? I thought the young lady likely dropped her diamonds at the accident. If you could have found them there – well, I am not eager to have so many thefts occur at my Rose and Thistle, Sir Edmund.'

Sir Edmund bestowed a few unflattering epithets on the man, but was too impatient to do him justice. 'Tote up my bill. Hurry!'

'Are you going after him?' Maisie asked Blount.

'Of course we are. Can you make it to my carriage, Miss Belmont?'

I did not think she was up to it, but she knew well enough I would go, and had no idea of letting me go off alone with Blount. She had her bonnet tied on her head before you could shake a stick, while I grabbed Mitzi up into my arms for a hasty exit. Blount's valet came to us, and was given instructions for the repair of our various carriages and the care of our nags. His groom was to be our driver. A wad of bills was stuffed into his hands, the whole affair done with the utmost haste and carelessness.

'Keep your eyes wide open here,' Blount instructed the man. 'If you see anything of a wall-eyed bastard in a green jacket, nab him. Frisk him, and don't let him away. He's stolen this lady's diamond necklace. But it's not likely he'll show his phiz back here.'

'Can't I go with you?' the man asked.

'Not this time. You are needed here. I'll be in touch with you. Come along, ladies.'

I felt a rising excitement, almost a joy, in the chase to come and the possibility of recovering my diamonds. I didn't forget them this time. Sir Edmund put a hand under both Maisie's and my elbows, one of us on either side of him, and rushed us out the door, while Mitzi hissed and spat at him. You would think we were headed to a fire, to hear Blount order the coachman to spring 'em, and keep his whip out.

CHAPTER 4

*D*espite Blount's cavalier dismissal of his brother's wedding, I took the idea it was preying on his mind, as we careened down the roads at a precarious speed. He kept glancing at his watch, frowning, drumming his fingers on his knees and showing other signs of stressful thought.

'Do you think we'll overtake the stage?' Maisie asked him.

'We might,' he answered indifferently, then looked at his watch again. 'The thing is done by now,' he announced sadly. 'The wedding. Poor Willie is shackled, a tenant for life.'

'Who is that, Sir Edmund?' Maisie asked. She was told in a few clipped phrases the awful fate of Willie Blount.

'You are against marriage, are you?' she asked, with some interest.

'Naturally,' he replied, astonished at her question.

Mitzi's dislike of Blount continued as the trip progressed. Having shimmied down from my lap to hold her paws against the window from the seat, she chose that moment to fall to the floor and to taste Sir Edmund's boots. He raised a hand to cuff her away. I rescued her in the nick of time, pulled her back on my lap while she wiggled in resistance.

'You and Lizzie are alike in that respect,' Maisie informed Blount. 'Being against marriage, I mean.'

'Lizzie? You refer to Miss Braden?' he verified, though he must have heard her call me so a dozen times that morning.

'Elizabeth is my name,' I said, with a repressive stare at Maisie, who knows I hate Lizzie, such a common, vulgar-sounding name.

'I had not realized, from your comments about my brother's match, that you were against marriage,' he said to me. 'Most ladies think it the reason they were put on the earth, to trap some fellow and make him their reason for living.'

'I am much too selfish for that,' I answered.

'Aye, she accepted the dog, but turned the gentleman down flat,' Maisie told him, shaking her head at Mitzi. 'Her last suitor made her a present of her pug.'

'No doubt you made a wise choice,' was Sir Edmund's only comment. He was not curious enough to inquire for the suitor's name. E'er long, his bad temper resurfaced, to be vented on the poor springing of the hired carriage, the inferior speed and uneven gait of the team, the condition of the roads and finally on the state of his stomach.

'We shall stop for luncheon at Andover,' he decided, 'and see if we cannot get a better team while there. These old jades are ready for the pound.' He hired a private parlor, and requested me to order his and our own luncheon while he went to select the team for the next lap. In the interest of a peaceful meal, I left Mitzi with the groom.

'What would you like to eat?' I asked him.

'Beefsteak and ale.'

'Anything else?'

'That is all I ever eat. Have it three times a day, for breakfast, lunch and dinner.'

'How very unimaginative!' I exclaimed, meaning no offense, but only blurting out the truth. He made some monosyllabic comment, which I did not quite hear, nor did I ask him to repeat it, for he looked cross.

His spirits had improved when he returned. 'I have borrowed a prime pair of grays from a friend I met at the stable. They have not gone above two miles, fresh as rain. He planned to leave them here overnight. We'll have a comfortable drive the rest of the way.'

The ale too was to his liking. He became so sociable while we awaited our food I thought for a moment he was going to smile. 'Paying a family visit to Fareham, are you, ladies?'

'Partly visit, partly business,' I answered. 'I was taking my necklace to sell to my uncle. They are interesting antiques, having come to my family directly from Queen Elizabeth hundreds of years ago.'

'Show him the box,' Maisie suggested, which I did.

He was mildly interested in the story. 'Why on earth would you *sell* such a rare family treasure?' he asked. 'These must be priceless to you, for sentimental, historical reasons alone.'

'Uncle Weston is the real historian of the family,' I answered, not wishing to stress our financial position. 'He has been after them any time these twenty years.'

'He likes them so well he had a copy made up a decade ago,' Maisie rattled on. 'He has all manner of artifact from those ancient times. In fact, his whole house is an antique. So is he. The windows in the place are of such old glass you can't see a thing through them – everything is blurred and uneven. The lawn looks like a pitching green lake.'

'I prefer modern architecture myself. So you capitulated, Miss Braden, and decided to sell him the diamonds. I hope you got a good price out of him.'

'Of course,' I said briefly.

'She would have got better had she sold them three years ago, when he offered. Now that we need the money, he is only offering thirty-five hundred,' Maisie detailed.

'Four thousand,' I corrected, quoting my own price.

'He said thirty-five hundred.'

'What was the original offer?' Blount asked.

'Five thousand,' Maisie replied.

'Antiques usually appreciate with age, not depreciate,' he pointed out.

'They depreciate with the need of the seller,' Maisie said bluntly. She was impervious to my quelling glances. I saw no reason to burden a stranger with our intimate family problems.

'I would not conclude the sale at this time, if I were you,' he advised.

'Till we recover the diamonds, it is academic,' I reminded them, hoping to quit this topic.

Maisie, having a keen listener, chose to go into the whole exposition of our situation: the prematurely cut forest, the cattle fever, the mortgage, right down to shillings and pence.

'I was wondering if you were *those* Bradens,' he said in a thin voice. Our infamy had risen as far north as Gloucester, as I feared.

'Yes, the unlucky ones,' Maisie told him, with something that sounded like perverse pride. Of course she was a Belmont, and was proffering all the gloom as my story. 'It is the lack of a man about the estate that accounts for our woes,' she ran on. 'Jeremy is only a young fellow, with no interest in anything but books. We got one bad steward after another. The one her Uncle Weston hired for us last has proven the worst of the lot. He *really* bankrupted us.'

'Weston Braden hired the spoiler, you mean?' he asked, one black brow rising in suspicion. 'The same Weston who wishes to acquire the diamonds at a reduced price?'

'Yes, the same, and there is no cause and effect between the two events, if that is what you are thinking, Sir Edmund,' I answered quickly, before Maisie turned inventive and made our case even more melodramatic than it already was. 'He is like Jeremy, interested in history and studies, not in farming. He certainly did not send Berrigan to us to relieve us of our money so we would sell him the necklace cheaply. He is not a scoundrel after all, my father's own brother.'

'I never liked him, nor his grinning stepson either,' Maisie averred.

I was happy to see the steaming plates being carried to

the table. I hoped the two of them would eat heartily and forget the misfortunes of Lizzie Braden.

Blount wore a greedy smile as his eyes surveyed five or ten pounds of beef, sitting in a pool of pan gravy. His knife went into it easily, indicating a pleasing tenderness. I could not account for the frown he suddenly put on. He cut deeper, pulled the meat apart with his knife and fork and bellowed for the servant, who was just leaving the room.

'This meat is burned black!' he said angrily, yet my eyes told me the delicious-looking morsel was pale pink inside, just turning to beige round the edges.

'It looks perfect,' I told him.

'I particularly asked for rare meat. Did you tell the waiter I wanted it rare?' he asked me.

'I didn't hear you say rare.' I had a memory of some unheard word, just as he was leaving.

'Take it away. No one could eat this charred stuff. Bring me a *rare* piece of beef,' he ordered. 'Just seared on the outside. I want it to bleed when I cut it.'

An involuntary shiver went through me. You remember, perhaps, my aversion to blood? The servant took the plate away. 'At least we won't have to wait long for a replacement. How long do you like your beefsteak to be cooked? Two seconds?'

'Closer to sixty. Thirty on either side – just seared, to hold in the juices. Pray do not wait for me, ladies. There is no need for you to eat cold food because they choose to serve burned leather in this place. Though how anyone can eat dead bird is beyond me,' he added, with a look of distaste at our fowl, which tasted suddenly very like dead bird.

'You have a lively manner of describing, Sir Edmund,' I complimented, pushing my plate away.

'I'll order you a nice beefsteak when the man comes back,' he tempted.

'No, really, wounded cow is no more appetizing to me than dead bird. I shall have some bread and butter. At least it never crowed or mooed.'

'The butter did,' he felt called upon to remind me.

'As I was saying about Weston Braden's stepson, Sir Edmund,' Maisie went on, undismayed by our host's atrocious manners, 'he is a handsome ne'er-do-well. Weston up and married the lad's mother, a widow young enough to be his daughter, some seven years ago.'

'You don't have to convince Sir Edmund of the folly of marriage, Aunt,' I pointed out.

They both ignored me. 'We all thought she would bury him in jig time and inherit his money, but it was no such a thing,' she continued. ' 'Twas himself who buried her two years ago, and who will get his fortune? Her lad, Glandower Cummings, that is who, cutting our poor Jeremy out entirely.'

'It seems Jeremy is unable to handle one estate, let alone two,' Blount said. He was back into his vile mood, due to the lateness of his meal.

'Glandower will get everything else, too,' she went on, undaunted. 'He'll end up with all the Elizabethan things. Lizzie's diamonds will sit around the neck of God only knows who – some cit's daughter, or worse. There is *one* marriage I have no sympathy with at least – Weston Braden's and Mrs. Cummings's. It was bad news for us.'

'What age is this Glandower fellow?' Blount asked.

'Twenty-five or thereabouts, wouldn't you say, Lizzie?'

'About that, yes.'

'He sounds a good match for you, Miss Braden,' he suggested.

'Ah, well, when she turned down *Lord* Beattie, it is not likely she would be taking up with a grinner like Cummings,' Maisie told him.

'You are truly devoted to the monastic life, to have rejected *Lord* Beattie,' he congratulated me. 'Is this the same Lord Beattie who resides at Eastgate?' he asked, with a suspicious twitching of the lips.

'That's the one. Do you know him?' she asked.

'Very slightly. He was a good friend of my grandfather. I am more closely acquainted with his son.'

'I shall take Mitzi for a walk while you two finish your carrion,' I said, arising on an impulse.

'*Finish* it? I wish I might *start* it! Here is the servant, at last,' he exclaimed.

I was vexed with Maisie for being so forthcoming with Sir Edmund. She is usually close-lipped with the neighbors, but there is often less constraint in our conversation when we are amongst strangers. I suppose it is knowing that we will not have to see them again that accounts for it. We need not care for the opinion of those who are nothing to us, still I disliked her readiness to gossip. I would speak to her about it, in a polite way.

I put Mitzi on her leash and took her for a walk along the main street of Andover, while I awaited for the two carnivores to finish their meal. It occurred to me I might encounter my dashing colonel, as he was also headed to Winchester, but I saw nothing of him. The afternoon was wearing well along when we remounted the carriage, but with the new team of grays, we made good time. It was our hope to arrive at Winchester in time to meet the coach, and apprehend the wall-eyed person in the green jacket as he descended. Sir Edmund felt that with the new team, there would be no difficulty in doing it as the stage stops so often, and sets such a sluggish pace.

Perhaps he was correct. If Maisie's ankle had not begun 'pulsating,' as she described its condition, we might have made it. She started twitching restlessly in her seat, then leaning down to massage the ankle, or to try to loosen the bandage. I don't know what she was doing down there, but I knew she must be in discomfort.

'Let's have a look at it,' Blount said, after glancing at her gyrations a few times.

Maisie has her fair share of maidenly modesty. '*You* take a look, Lizzie,' she said, with a little blush.

'Shall I don a blindfold, or will you be satisfied if I just look out the window, Maisie?' he teased. The two of them had achieved a first-name basis back at the inn while I walked Mitzi. God only knows what other family secrets she told him.

'Promise you won't peek,' she answered, in accents worthy of a coquette. He turned obediently to look out the window as I lifted her leg up, to see the ankle mushrooming to an enormous size, with the bandage put on at Devizes cutting into the swelling.

'Good God! This has got to come off! Sir Edmund, look

at this!' I was too worried to honor her wish for modesty.

He looked around. His eyes grew wider as he reached down to touch the swelling with an exploratory finger. 'We have got to get you to a sawbones, Maisie,' he said at once.

'What about the Winchester stage? We don't want to miss it. If we don't overtake the wall-eyed fellow there, we won't know where to look for him. Though it *does* hurt. It pulses, like a heart, you know.'

'It must be the bandage that causes it. It can't be infection. There is no open wound. I'll loosen it for you.' He pulled off the plaster that held the bandage on, and unwound the cotton. The discoloration was visible through her silk stocking. It looked as if she had a red cabbage stuffed down her leg.

'Forget the Winchester stage and the diamonds for the moment, Maisie. We shall stop at the first signs of civilization and look for a doctor,' I said. Sir Edmund nodded his agreement.

We were not very far from a village called Testley. We pulled in at the inn there, hired a room and sent off for the local doctor. While awaiting him, we made her as comfortable as possible by propping her sore ankle up on a footstool, opening windows, getting wine and so on. Before long the doctor entered, a bald little man with glasses and a speckled skull.

He did not immediately see Maisie, reclining in the corner, and mistook me for the patient, as I wore the patch on my temple. 'What seems to be the trouble, young lady?' he asked with abominable cheer. 'A migraine, I wager.'

'No, my aunt has a wrenched ankle,' I informed him, pointing out her chair.

Sir Edmund and I went to the other side of the largish chamber to await his verdict. 'You should have him take a look at your bruise while he is here,' he suggested.

'Nature is the best healer. The less I have doctors tampering with me, the better I like it. I shall get some headache drops from him before he leaves though.'

'Is it bothering you?' he asked, with a little show of concern.

'Of course it is. You do not sustain such a blow without suffering.'

'That would account for your irritable temper. I fear what I am about to say will exacerbate it.

'Don't say it then,' I advised, but he spoke on.

'Has it occurred to you this fellow with the wall-eye that we are chasing is wending his way very close to Fareham?'

'Yes, and I am very happy for it. He is not taking us much out of our way. After we have overtaken him, we can go along to Fareham, we'll be practically there. Maisie and I can go on, I mean.'

'You see no significance in the coincidence?'

'I do not see that Weston put him up to stealing it, if *that* is the meaning of your questions.'

'Your aunt does not share your good opinion of him.'

'My aunt and I often disagree as to what constitutes a pleasing character. She is only unhappy that he married Mrs. Cummings. My family does not harbor any criminals, Sir Edmund. Weston will be horrified when he hears what has happened to us.'

'Very well, if you say so. I felt obliged to mention it. Forgive me if I have offended you.'

'That is quite all right. I am under no illusion as to who put this idea in your head.'

'I have another suggestion which will be more pleasing than my last,' he continued. 'I recommend you remain here with your aunt, while I go on and meet the stage at Winchester, have the thief arrested and return your necklace to you.'

'You would not recognize my necklace to see it,' I answered, finding him totally wrong in his opinion that I would like this second suggestion. I was disappointed to see our adventure be cut off so abruptly.

'It is not likely the man will have more than one set of diamonds in his pocket.'

'His profession is stealing. Heaven only knows how many he has picked up by now.'

'Surely not more than one dating back to the reign of Queen Elizabeth,' he countered. 'I really ought to be getting on for Winchester.'

'My aunt is looking very chipper,' I pointed out. 'She will be ready to travel.' She was revived enough to be joking with the doctor.

'She is a game old girl, is she not?' he answered, smiling toward the corner.

'Up to all the rigs. It would be a shame to deprive her of the chase.' He drew out his watch. I knew what was on his mind, but hoped to divert his attention till the doctor was through with Maisie.

'You are ruing your brother's fate again, are you? He

would be off on his wedding trip by now, I expect.'

'No need to pity him the honeymoon at least. I am going to pester the doctor into a hurry. He is making a career out of a sprained ankle. He's had that bandage on and off a dozen times.'

He walked across the room to do as he had said, but the fault was not all with the doctor. Maisie, certainly happy from an excess of wine, had developed an unusual flair for attention. It was too tight, then too loose, and when at length it was adjusted to her pleasure, she found she required a cane to assist her walking. Full weight caused the pulsating to set in again, or so she imagined.

'Oh, Maisie! I wish you had told us sooner. I could have run out and bought one while you were being tended. This will hold us up – and the Winchester coach will be getting in soon.'

Even as I spoke, Sir Edmund flew out the door, to return a minute later with a blackthorn walking stick purchased from a customer at the tap-room. This he presented to my aunt with great ceremony, while he simultaneously looked at the clock on the wall and pulled her up from the chair.. With Blount for a cane on her other side, she hobbled to the carriage without too much difficulty. We piled in, then it was my turn to delay us.

'Where is Mitzi?' I asked the driver, who had been charged with watching her.

'Lord love us, has that mutt sneaked off again?' he asked, scratching his head. 'I've spent the past half hour chasing her all over town.'

'Leave her behind,' Blount suggested impatiently.

'Leave Mitzi?' I asked, astonished at his lack of sensitivity.

'We can pick her up on the way back,' Maisie told me.

'Pick her up where? She won't stay here. Someone will steal her. I must find her.'

'I'll wait in the carriage,' my aunt said. 'My ankle is starting its pulsing again.'

'Sir Edmund – if you would help me, it would go more quickly. I'll go east, you go west,' I said, trying to entice him with a smile.

'Try that dirty-looking river down yonder,' Maisie advised us. 'Mitzi loves water, the dirtier, the better.'

It was, unfortunately, true. I took the road to the river, while Sir Edmund, muttering under his breath, went the other way. Mitzi was enjoying a paddle out after a stick which some urchins were tossing for her when I found her. She came leaping toward me eagerly enough, shaking dirty water in all directions, with a deal of it landing on my good jonquil muslin. I grabbed her leash to hasten back to the carriage.

Sir Edmund had done precious little chasing. He stood drumming his fingers against the carriage door, looking at his watch. 'You realize there is no possibility of meeting the stage, Lizzie?' he asked irritably.

As I was feeling culpable in the latest delay, I did not deem it the propitious moment to reprimand him for using my hated nickname.

'If we hurry, we might,' I replied, opening the door myself, as he made no motion of doing so.

'Just a minute!' He reached over my shoulder to push

the door shut. 'I am not sharing a carriage with a wet, smelly, bad-tempered bitch.'

'You want me to sit on the box?' I asked, though of course I knew he referred to Mitzi. I hoped I might joke her way inside.

He was more shocked than amused at my poor attempt at a jest, but not shocked enough to lose track of his intention. The dog was removed from my custody and handed up to the coachman, who was instructed to lose the mutt if he could.

Maisie was disgusted with me. 'What will Edmund think of you?' she asked. Edmund was still outside the carriage, speaking to the driver.

'If a man cannot take a joke, I don't care what he thinks of me.'

I did not think he heard, but as he sat stiff as a judge for full ten minutes once we finally got moving, I began to alter my opinion. He had heard all right, and was displeased.

CHAPTER 5

*O*ur first stop at Winchester was the coaching office to inquire whether the stage had come in. When we learned it had arrived a quarter of an hour before us, we questioned a few employees and loiterers for information regarding the green-jacketed man. We received two confirmations that such an individual had alit, but no clue as to his destination.

'It will be best for you to see to your aunt's comfort while I go and make more inquiries,' Sir Edmund decided. 'We'll hire a parlor at the inn and order some wine.'

'Let her sober up from the last onslaught of wine before you order more,' I suggested. We were not accustomed to drinking so much wine throughout the day.

'My head is aching. I wouldn't mind a lie down,' Maisie told him.

'How is the ankle? Still pulsating?' he inquired.

'No, now it's my head that's banging like a hammer.' The wine – definitely she had drunk too much wine.

I saw no necessity to sit and watch Maisie snore off her

tipple. 'I shall go with you,' I told Sir Edmund.

'I have no idea where my inquiries might lead me. It is possible I may end up at some haunts where a lady would not be comfortable,' he objected.

'Very well, then I shall go alone to the less objectionable spots. I can visit the pawn shops.'

'Alone?' he asked, blinking in disapproval.

'No, with Mitzi.'

'It is early yet to start visiting pawn shops. The man has hardly had time to lay your necklace on the shelf. I planned to go to a few inns, step into the taprooms, take a quick walk down the street. The coach has only been in a quarter of an hour. He might be just walking around to get the kinks out of his legs after the trip.'

'Your itinerary does not sound too disreputable for a lady. I could wait in the inn lobbies while you enter the taprooms.'

He hesitated only a moment. When he spoke, it came out it was Mitzi's company he objected to, and not my own. I do not mention it on every page, but when Mitzi was in our company, she was making a terrific nuisance of herself, growling and hissing at Sir Edmund, for whom she had an infinite contempt.

'I'll leave her behind,' I offered. 'I was only taking her along to replace you. I mean. . . .'

'Thank you,' he said, his lips thinning noticeably. He went to the desk to hire the room for Maisie. We helped her upstairs, left Mitzi with her and went out into the street.

Our search was not fruitful. Sir Edmund, if I have not

mentioned it, was a tall man, with legs approximately three feet long. He moved them very fast, with no concern for a companion hampered by flopping skirts and legs twelve inches shorter than his own. I fairly ran down one side of the main street and up the other. If I uttered a word of objection, I would be invited to retire to the inn. I regained my breath when we began making inquiries at all the possible stops of a pickpocket. It was possible for me to stand or sit in a lobby, depending on the quality of the establishment visited, while Blount made his inquiries.

A moss green jacket is not at all a stylish thing; gentlemen wear a blue one; farmers and workers wear all colors, but a surprising number of green jackets turned up on the street to attract our attention that day. A dozen times we made a useless dart across the road or into a shop, lured by a green outfit. 'We should have got a closer description of him. We don't know whether he is tall or short, what sort of a hat he wears – nothing but the jacket and the wall-eye,' I repined. 'Colonel Fortescue probably left a perfectly accurate description of him, too, as he was so thoughtful as to run back to the inn and inform the innkeeper of the man's destination.'

'Maisie saw him. He's a small fellow, both short and thin, spindly shanked, she called him.' Blount's conversation was never what one would call dulcet-toned. When the colonel's name arose, it became even more brusque. Maisie hinted it was because I was forever singing the fellow's praises, but I only mentioned him at appropriate moments, no matter how often I *thought* of him.

After we had been searching for over an hour, I

suggested our man, whom we had nicknamed Greenie in order to refer to him briefly, had had time to sell the diamonds. 'Let us begin checking the pawn shops now. There is a sign across the road.' We hastened across to the sign of the three globes, just as the proprietor walked out the door and turned the key in the lock, his day's business done. We asked him about Greenie, but he shook his head uninterestedly.

'I didn't see anyone like that,' he said, strolling off towards a tavern.

'He wouldn't tell us if he had bought them. He knows perfectly well they are stolen,' I said. 'If Greenie is a regular pickpocket, he probably has a man who handles his wares for him. A fence they call it, I believe.'

'That is possible. I'll have to find my way to the wrong side of town tonight, and begin making discreet inquiries.'

This sounded highly exciting. I knew I would not be allowed to accompany him on so degrading an errand unless I came up with an extraordinary plan. While I schemed, wishing I had a set of livery or a boy's outfit to slip into, Sir Edmund turned his blighting eyes on me and shook his head. 'Forget it, Miss Braden. I will be going alone. We'll have dinner now, to allow me an early start.'

We had worked our way back close to our inn. I was hungry enough to welcome the thought of dinner, and venturesome enough to continue plotting how I might get myself included in the night's work. I was sent upstairs to see if Maisie wished to come down to dinner, or we should eat above-stairs with her. She was sufficiently bored with her incarceration that she would tackle the stairs, with the aid of her walking stick and a strong arm from Sir Edmund. No fancy dressing was possible, with our trunks at Devizes, but as Blount hired a private parlor, it did not matter. Mitzi was left behind in the room, highly pleased with the arrangement.

'I'll bring something up for her after dinner. I shall have to take her for a walk too, before she is shut in for the night,' I mentioned.

'I cannot imagine why any sane person goes traveling with a dog,' Edmund said curtly.

I opened my lips to make some excuse, but he was no longer heeding me. His eyes had wandered down to the bottom of the stairs. His expression was one of such lively delight I had not a doubt in the world I would see a green jacket below us, in the lobby. I followed his line of gaze, to view not a wall-eyed man, but a very buxom female in a low-cut gown, casting a provocative smile in his direction. Lightskirts are finding their way into even the better class of public inn these days. This one was enough to ruin the reputation of the place, to say nothing of its clients' morals. She was a sultry-eyed, raven-haired hussy, giving wanton encouragement to every scarecrow in the place. Certainly nothing else but a member of the muslin company. She was accompanied by an elderly female, who was posing as a chaperone, which was only a ruse to get herself inside the door. They would never have let this one in unaccompanied. The two of them were entering a private parlor, and taking their sweet time to do it too, as the response from Blount was so very promising for business.

I had not taken him for a lecher. That breed of male is usually much more amusing. His manners were businesslike, brusque to the point of rudeness. Then too he professed moral opinions on such matters as thievery, to say nothing of his virulent misogamy. After the female's door had closed, he stood staring at the wooden panels with a bemused look on his face.

'Shall we continue on, or would you like to make a closer examination of the door?' I asked politely.

His head jerked quickly toward me. 'A pretty woman,' he remarked, trying to make it sound casual. 'I shouldn't be surprised if she is an actress.'

'I took her profession for something older. The world's oldest, in fact.'

He busied himself holding the door for us, to obviate replying. While he ordered up his raw meat, Maisie and I settled on tastier fare. 'No dead birds for me tonight,' I decided, running an eye down the long menu. 'I shall begin with dead fish instead.'

Maisie t'sked in annoyance, and ordered an exact replica of my own dinner, despite Sir Edmund's remonstrances that what we both needed was a nice, rare piece of beefsteak. The only variation in our host's repast was that he switched to wine from ale. He was careful to warn them how to sear his meat. The blood oozed just as he liked when he put his knife into it. By a careful rearrangement of the flower vase on our table, I was able to conceal this disgusting spectacle from my eyes. Over dinner, we outlined to Maisie what had occupied us earlier, and our lack of success.

'Sir Edmund is going to visit criminal haunts tonight, to try to find the fence,' I explained.

We did not dally over our meal. There was never a chance to dally over anything, with Blount forever pulling out his watch and urging us to eat up. Before I had finished scalding my interior by trying to drink the boiling coffee, Edmund was pushing back his chair, outlining that he must be off to the wrong side of town.

'I must walk Mitzi now, and beg a scrap of meat from the kitchen for her.'

'You cannot go out alone. It is nearly dark,' he informed me. 'I'll have one of the inn boys walk her for you.'

'There is time to walk her a block up and down the main street before dark. I am not likely to be accosted on the main street of Winchester.'

'Very well, if you *insist*, I shall have to accompany you,' he told me, his hackles rising.

'Don't be ridiculous. I always do this when we are traveling.'

'You never took Mitzi away from home before,' Maisie pointed out, with hateful and unnecessary accuracy.

I went upstairs to get Mitzi. My aunt had decided to remain in the private parlor while we walked the dog. She would finish her coffee at leisure, lucky aunt. Whom should I run into in the lobby but Colonel Fortescue! We greeted each other as long lost friends.

'What a small world it is! Miss Braden – delightful to meet you again. I was wrong to accuse Fate of perversity, was I not?' The colonel was in evening clothes, looking criminally attractive. I felt the strongest urge to drag him into the parlor to meet Blount, to show him how a proper gentleman looked and behaved.

'Colonel Fortescue! Did you get your watch back?' Glancing to his waistcoat, I saw by the chain he had. He was resourceful on top of all the rest.

'Certainly I did. You heard of it at the inn in Devizes?'

'Heard of it? Oh, you don't know, Colonel! I too was robbed.' I outlined my ill-fated tale to him. He was hot in his sympathy. Somehow or other, he got hold of my hands, squeezed them tightly. 'If only I had *known*! To think, I had the culprit right in my hands, and let him go. Is there anything I can do to help you?'

'The best help you can give is to tell me where you found your watch. Did you meet the fellow as he got off the coach?'

'I did. I arrived in advance of him.'

'Was he not taken into custody?'

'Alas, no! Had I had the least notion what a wretched fellow he is, I would have done it. But I felt sorry for the poor devil. Only a drifter. I arranged the business quietly with him, got my watch, and let him off with a warning.'

'You are too soft-hearted.'

'Foolishly kind, as it turns out. I feel as guilty as though I had robbed you of your diamonds myself. How can I assist you?'

'You don't happen to know where the scoundrel is headed?'

'I only know he darted down the street as fast as his spindly legs would carry him. Probably had a customer waiting for your hot stones. I insist on helping you. I am yours to command, Miss Braden.' He stopped suddenly, striking his forehead with his fingers, rather like a salute. 'Oh, dear. The trouble is, I am *not* free to help you. I must be in London before morning. I was about to climb into my curricle this very minute and get back on the road.'

'That is a pity, but the gentleman who caused my accident is giving every assistance. Have you time to step into the parlor yonder and make his acquaintance?'

'I wish I had, but this business of my watch has held me up so long. I have to get to London tonight. I really must dash off. I suppose it is folly to hope you have changed your destination?' he asked, with a rather shy smile.

'I'm afraid it is.'

'I was right the first time. She *is* perverse. Fate, I mean.' He looked at me with those long-fringed eyes. There was regret in them, and if there was not the same expression in mine I would be much mistaken. He bowed, turned and left. Mitzi, showing great discrimination, had been well-behaved throughout the meeting.

I turned back to our parlor, then realized I had removed my spencer and would want it for the walk, so darted back to our room to get it. When I descended, the sultry-eyed female had emerged from her parlor and had cornered Sir Edmund. She was talking to him, batting her lashes, smiling. She lifted her head like a duchess when I approached, and ducked back into her parlor, as she had not time to get out of my view in any other direction.

'I thought she might possibly have seen Greenie,' Blount explained, with a sheepish look.

'Had she?'

'I hadn't time to inquire. She mistook you for my wife – was just asking about you.'

'I trust you told her you are a confirmed misogamist.'

'Somehow, the matter did not arise. I had not time to make her any proposal, you see.'

'Only a proposition? Or does she handle the business details herself?'

I do not know whether his glare was for my question or Mitzi's querulous snapping at his boots. 'Let's get out of here before the mutt disgraces us,' he suggested.

As we went toward the door I said, 'As it happens, I have learned Greenie was in town. I met Colonel Fortescue in the lobby just a moment ago.'

'You should have brought him in to meet us. I would like to see the paragon.'

I gave a wistful sigh. 'Unfortunately, he was in a great rush to get to London. I don't suppose I shall ever see him again. Two ships that pass in the night. . . .'

'Did the ship have anything useful to tell you?'

I outlined Fortescue's information as we strolled along the main thoroughfare, our chore of walking the dog requiring a leisurely pace.

'The idiot!' Sir Edmund muttered. 'Hadn't the wits to have the jackanapes arrested.'

'He is too soft-hearted. I told him so. He was very upset about it.'

'I expect that was enough to make him break into tears.'

'No, he is too manly for tears. A veteran, you know, wounded.'

'In the Peninsula,' he added.

We kept an eye peeled for Greenie. Colors were still discernible, though everything was turning to gray rather rapidly. Mitzi, whom I had not fed yet, kept her nose to the ground for food and found a crust of bread against a shop wall. I tried to tug her away from it, but she held firm, necessitating my going closer to lift her away.

'This is a pawn shop,' Sir Edmund mentioned, as these establishments were of particular interest to us. 'We must try it in the morning, if my search is not successful tonight.'

'Yes, close to the coach stop, too. He might well have unloaded his loot here.' I glanced into the window, and emitted a shriek. 'Sir Edmund! That's it! There, right in the middle of the window – my diamond necklace.'

He nearly put his head through the glass in his excitement. He leaned against the windowpane, as I did myself, to verify my jewelry. 'Funny the man would put such a valuable thing in the window – vulnerable. Anyone could break the glass and steal it. You'll notice the other objects are not really worth much. Watches, fans, hats. . . . No genuine jewelry but yours.'

'He probably thinks it is strass glass. Maybe Greenie thought so when he sold it.'

'No, the dealer would know what he was about, if the pickpocket did not. I don't think those are real diamonds, Miss Braden.'

'Of course they are. He hasn't had time to pry them out and make paste replicas. We must get them. What's the name of the place?'

'Reuben's Pawn Shop,' he read, standing back to crane

his neck up to the sign. 'We'll come here first thing tomorrow morning.'

'Tomorrow morning?' I asked. 'We cannot leave them here all night. You said yourself they could easily be stolen. We must find out where Reuben lives, and go to his place. He'll have to come back and let us in.'

'It can wait till morning. They are safe enough.'

'I don't intend to leave them here over night.'

'I have other plans for my evening.'

'Not now! It is no longer necessary to find your way to the wrong side of town, to look for the fence person.'

'Those were not the plans I referred to.'

'I see. You refer to the bit of the wrong side of town that has registered at the inn, do you? You are a fast worker, Sir Edmund.'

'I will not stir a finger to find Reuben this night,' he answered.

I am very happy to relate Mitzi defended me. She never likes to hear anyone speak roughly to me. She jumped up and sunk her teeth into his boots. Had he been wearing pantaloons, he would have felt it.

'And we're getting rid of this foul-natured bitch too!' he threatened, shaking her off.

CHAPTER 6

$\mathcal{M}$itzi accompanied us on our expedition to find Mr Reuben, as soon as we returned to the inn to tell Maisie of our plan and seen her to the room abovestairs. As it was getting so late, Sir Edmund booked rooms for us all to remain overnight. Even before returning to the inn, we learned Mr Reuben's residence from a small coffee shop next door. The proprietor, as I pointed out to Sir Edmund, was bound to know him, from having done business in the neighboring shop. It would take a Sir Edmund to insist it was utterly unlikely the two shopkeepers had ever spoken to each other over the years.

The coffee shop keeper knew all about Reuben. 'He don't live just around the corner,' he told us. 'Reuben, he lives out of town, and comes in each morning on his mule. Down Churchhouse Walk you'll find him. Take the road out of town a mile, turn left and follow the footpath that meanders all crinkum-crankum another half mile or more. Reuben lives in the shack place you'll come to. There hard by the stream you'll find him. Mind he may not be sober, so late in the day.'

'Thank you,' Sir Edmund said, disliking the inconvenience of the location. The proprietor was unhappy, too, to receive no *pourboire* for his help.

I nudged Blount's arm. He glanced at me, frowning. 'Give him something,' I said in a low voice.

'What?'

'*Pay* him. Give him a tip.'

'Oh!' He reached into his pocket and pulled out a coin of a denomination that was much too large. The man bit it before tossing it into his change box.

'There is obviously no point in going tonight,' Sir Edmund said, when we left the coffee shop. 'His shack way to hell in the woods somewhere, and he dead drunk by now.'

'She'll wait for you, Sir Edmund.'

'That is *not* why I refuse to go. We'll wait till morning.'

'If I must go alone at night, I hope you will at least loan me your carriage and a boy to accompany me,' I answered.

'Miss Braden,' he began in a frustrated, holding-back-his-temper kind of a way.

'That is quite all right. Mitzi will come with me. How I wish Colonel Fortescue were here.' I lifted Mitzi into my arms as we headed back to the inn. 'Poor girl,' I said. 'Bad Lizzie hasn't given you any dinner. You shall have a nice beefsteak for a reward.' She cooed softly, then turned her head aside to snap at Blount, who was muttering into his collar.

'Shut up!' he shouted to the dog, as he was not quite

rude enough to say it to me.

Reuben's roost was neither far away nor difficult to find. The only little impediment was that once we reached the crinkum-crankum path, we had to descend and leave the carriage behind, to proceed on foot. The innocent foot-path was castigated as everything from a jungle to a bog by my surly companion. The nettles *did* cling tenaciously to my skirts, though they were less bothersome to his booted feet. The occasional puddle we slipped into may have soaked my slippers, but cannot have done much damage to his Hessians.

Reuben was almost sober when we arrived. He had a large bottle of cheap wine at his elbow, but had not drunk more than the half of it. He was alert enough to demand a stiff price for obliging us in the business. He looked like a wizened, spiteful elf. He had black hair that had receded in two moons from a narrow face. His eyes were black, his nose sharp, his teeth mostly missing. They were repre-sented by two eyeteeth on top, and one front projection on the bottom. Chewing, I should think, was impossible for him, which might account for his liquid diet.

'A body don't like to be pelting all the way back into town at the end of a hard day. What will happen is that I'll be too fagged to go back in the morning. Miss a half day's earnings.' He sniffed, and lifted his dirty tumbler to his lips.

'How much?' Sir Edmund asked.

'No saying either when we get there that the diamonds will be them you're after. Very fine diamonds they are. I paid the wall-eyed feller a hundred guineas for them.'

'They're worth a lot . . .' Edmund began. I gave his

ankle a sharp kick to hush him up, before the man tumbled to it they were worth fifty times that sum. 'Why did you leave them in the window, if they are so valuable?' he asked instead.

'To lure in the carriage trade,' Reuben answered, with a challenging light in his black eyes. 'Yessir, I paid him one hundred guineas. Then there'll be the half day's earnings to be made up. My valu'ble time yanked away from me.' He looked forlornly at the bottle. I reached out and removed it to the far side of the table.

Mitzi growled at him. 'Nice doggie,' Reuben said, then spat on the filthy floor, very close to her.

'We're in a hurry, Reuben,' Sir Edmund said. 'If you want to sell the necklace, you must come with us tonight. Now.'

'Take an hour to go, then to be coming back at midnight . . .'

'I'll stand you to a room at the inn. You can come in my carriage. The trip won't take long.'

After a half dozen more put-offs, Edmund resorted to saying the necklace was stolen anyway, and he would go to the constable if he had to wait till morning. This finally got Reuben up on his pegs. As it turned out, he had no intention of coming in our carriage. He hitched up his mule and arrived at his shop very shortly after we did ourselves. He made the trip down the crinkum-crankum path faster; we made up the time on the surfaced road. He let us into a pitch black shop, lit a few rush lights, then clambered into the window to get out the necklace. I reached out eagerly for it.

I knew as soon as I held it in my hands that it was not mine. It *looked* like it; the design was identical, but it did not *feel* like it. Seeing my puzzlement, Sir Edmund lifted it and carried it into a light.

'Got a loupe?' he asked Reuben.

He had one, but was reluctant to produce it. I soon knew why.

'These aren't diamonds,' Blount said, after a cursory examination.

'If they ain't, I was bilked out of a hundred guineas,' Reuben answered staunchly, while his black eyes began shifting around his crabbed, jumbled heap of a place.

'You were bilked,' Blount told him, quite jubilantly, thinking only of revenge and not of my plight. 'I am taking them next door to the coffee shop for a better light. Come along if you like.' Reuben accompanied him. As I had no wish to remain alone in his shop, I tagged along as well.

'Not even a good copy,' Blount said, tossing the necklace on to the table. 'These aren't worth a guinea.'

'One guinea? I paid two!' Reuben howled.

I exchanged a tacit look with Sir Edmund, who shook his head ruefully at the corruption of mankind. 'Do you want them?' he asked me.

'I don't know. Yes, they might be handy to show the Bow Street Runners what they are looking for, I suppose. I shall have to make a formal statement to them. We can't find the diamonds alone. We need help.'

The words sent Reuben into a tizzy. 'Don't be dragging the Runners down on my head. I want no truck with them. I don't know nothing about the wall-eyed feller who sold me the necklace. He laid the piece on the wood, said he had no more use for 'em and what price would they fetch. I give him two guineas, and that's all *I* know.'

'You said you gave him a hundred, and that they were diamonds,' I reminded him.

'Business,' he explained, as though I were a fool not to realize it. 'A man's got to make a living, don't he? I don't know nothing about diamonds. This gentleman *told* me they was diamonds. They could have been diamonds for all me or the wall-eyed feller knew. If it happened they *was*, why should I give them away for two guineas, eh?'

'Do you know anything about the fellow – have you dealt with him before?' Sir Edmund asked.

'I see him from time to time. He don't live in town, I'm pretty sure, but he can't live far from it. I see him maybe once a month. He hawks gimcrack stuff, not real jewels.'

'Watches, rings?' Edmund pressed on.

'No, I don't think he's a gallows bird. Not the sort of thing you'd snaffle from a fellow's pocket. A bit of lady's junk, but mostly house stuff. A small fancy table or picture. I allus reckoned he worked for gentry folks and did a bit of pilfering from the attic, where they'd not miss it.'

'If he shows up again, call the constable,' Blount ordered. 'Give them this card. I want to be notified.' He gave Reuben one of his cards.

'I will,' Reuben promised at once, but of course he would not. He would sooner call in Satan than the Law.

The glass necklace was paid for, with an extra guinea thrown in for his trouble. As we were going toward the door, Blount turned and went back toward Reuben, to have another word with him.

'What was that about?' I asked.

'I told him what hotel we are staying at, in case Greenie turns up at his door again. You've got the necklace, have you?'

'No, you've got it.'

'So I have,' he said, patting his pocket. He seemed a little distracted, but we were talking about the oddness of finding the replica in his shop, and I soon forgot it as we hastened toward the inn.

He accompanied me to Maisie's room. She was still up and dressed, so she invited him in. 'Did you get it?' she asked.

'No, it was only a copy,' he said, handing it to her. 'You're sure this isn't the one you brought from home?' he asked me.

'My original was heavier, much better made. This would not have fooled me, even through a window, if it had not been coming on dark.'

'You mentioned your Uncle Weston had a copy made some ten years ago.'

'Yes, this must be it,' I said, puzzling over it. 'I wonder if Greenie works for Uncle – pinched it from him.'

'I am bound to say that is not the interpretation *I* placed on it,' Sir Edmund disagreed. 'Reuben said the fellow lives not far from here. Fareham is not far from here. We know Greenie stole your necklace. We know he pawned a copy for which he had no more use – he told Reuben so. It looks to me as though your Uncle Weston gave him the copy to be able to identify the original and steal it. No one but your uncle knew you would have the necklace with you. Two ladies, unprotected on the open road, were an easy mark. If Greenie were only some chance pickpocket, he would not have had the copy. This was planned. He knew you were coming. How should he have known it if your uncle did not tell him? The accident facilitated the theft, of course, but I come to believe you would never have reached Fareham with it in any case.'

'I am sure my uncle had nothing to do with it!' I objected at once.

'*I* never liked him above half,' Maisie said, as though her personal preference had anything to do with it.

'You never thought he was a thief!' I pointed out scorn- fully.

'Maybe I didn't, but I'm not one bit surprised. He always coveted that necklace, Lizzie.'

'He offered to *pay* for it!'

'How could it have been done without his contrivance?' Blount asked, with a smug look on his face. 'It is too much coincidence that Greenie stole first the copy from your uncle, then the original from you. There is some connec- tion between the two.'

'No, there is not,' I insisted mulishly, though I was coming to wonder if he were not right. It was not far from dishonesty to shave fifteen hundred from the first price offered, when he knew I must accept it.

'What do you want to do?' Blount asked.

'I am going to a constable in the morning.'

'That you are not!' Maisie responded, huffing in indig- nation. 'A fine thing, dragging your uncle into court. It is best to settle it quietly.'

'I do not believe Weston is guilty.'

'If you mean that, why do you not go to him and tell him what has happened?' Sir Edmund suggested. 'It is possible he can throw some light on the matter. He may know something about the fellow in the green jacket.'

It sounded a sensible idea. 'Yes, I'll do that,' I answered.

'We shall continue on toward Wareham in the morning then?' he confirmed.

'There is no need for you to go any farther out of your way, Sir Edmund. I feel badly we have inconvenienced you as much as we have.'

'I have come this far. I might as well see it through to the end. Besides, you do not have a carriage.'

Maisie was looking around the room, frowning, while Edmund picked up the glass jewelry and stuck it into his pocket. 'Where is the dog?' she asked suddenly.

After having finally remembered to keep a thought on my diamonds, I had forgotten my dog. I could not remember having seen her since we were at Reuben's shop. 'Sir Edmund, we have left her at Reuben's, or the coffee shop. We must go and get her.'

'It is not far away. She'll find her way back,' he said.

'No, I must get her. In a strange place . . .'

I turned and dashed out the door. He came darting after me. 'Don't bother. She's not there,' he said.

'She has to be at one place or the other. I hope she is not locked in at Reuben's place. She'll have her little nose against the window, looking for me.' The forlorn image caused me to hurry my steps down the stairs, across the lobby.

At the doorway, Blount put up an arm to stop me. 'This is a wild goose chase. She'll be gone by now.'

'No, she won't. She's locked in. She'll be petrified. I must get her.'

I was suddenly aware of a wary, reluctant expression on his face. My concern for Mitzi had distracted my attention. 'She is not there,' he stated firmly.

'What do you mean? Sir Edmund, have you done something with her?' I demanded, suspicion rapidly shifting to certainty, as he grew more embarrassed by the moment.

'Reuben took her home,' he said, with a pugnacious lift of the chin, to try to hide his shame.

'Took her, or you gave her to him? That's why you went back to speak to him, wasn't it? You *sold* her to him!'

'*Sold* her? I had to give him another guinea to take her!'

'You *monster*!' I charged, in a loud, accusing voice.

The man behind the desk glanced up, disliking an altercation to greet his patrons at the doorway. 'Is there some trouble, ma'am?' he asked, with a leery glance toward Blount.

'Yes, there is something very much wrong. This – this *creature* stole my dog!'

'Is this true?' he asked Blount, in very timid accents.

'You might accept the word of a lady!' I told him, very much on my high ropes.

'I merely placed the dog with a friend, as I did not like having it snarling around the inn, disturbing the patrons,' Blount answered, making his reply pleasing to the clerk.

'She only snarls when you kick her!' I reminded him, with a stormy look.

'I did not *kick* her. Even when she bit my leg, I did not kick her.'

'If you would not mind, pray continue this spat in your room,' the clerk begged.

'I am not going to my room till I get Mitzi back.'

'*I* am not setting a toe out the door again tonight,' Blount replied.

'Very well, I shall go alone.'

'Not in *my* carriage you won't!'

'These marital squabbles are best conducted in private,' the poor clerk said, beginning to wring his hands in consternation.

'Marital squabbles? We are not married!' I said angrily, while Sir Edmund shouted something similar in a louder voice. I believe I heard the words 'the last woman in the world I would marry,' or something of the sort.

'Brothers and sisters are worse! Pray do not make a scene in public. The proprietor will be furious with me. It is my first night on the job,' the harried clerk implored. I could not squelch a shred of pity for the fellow.

I had to either storm out the door alone into the dark night, or turn tail and go back to my room without Mitzi. It was a hard decision to make. My pride urged me out the door, where Blount would surely follow, if he had any claims at all to the name of gentleman. Still, I was by no means certain he would follow, nor was I at all eager to repeat that long, annoying journey to Reuben's shack, certainly not on foot. I was tired, angry and becoming embarrassed as a few customers with nothing better to do had begun to clump themselves around us for the show.

'Very well, I shall leave Mitzi with that cruel, drunken crook for tonight, but if anything has happened to her by morning, Sir Edmund, I shall hold you personally responsible.'

'Nothing will happen to her,' he said, relieved at the squabble coming to this decent halt. 'I'll take you to your room now.'

I turned, stiff as a ramrod, to mount the stairs with him at my heels. His taste of victory proved sweet enough that he decided to push his luck a bit farther. 'Reuben is not cruel, and he is not a total drunkard. He is interested in keeping Mitzi, as a guard dog at his shack when he is at work. I thought we could leave her there permanently. She will be well cared for, happy as a grig, running around the fields all day. It is a perfect solution to this problem.'

'This *problem*, as you call it, is of your devising. I do not intend to leave Winchester without Mitzi. You are more than welcome to desert us. We can manage perfectly well without your helpful presence, overturning our carriage and creating scenes everywhere we go. If it is a choice between the two, I choose the dog. That rids us of the *real* problem.'

'As you wish,' he said, with a short bow, biting in all his vituperation, as there was a couple coming along the hallway.

He turned and went downstairs, his face tight and pink with anger, as I entered Maisie's room.

'What's eating you?' she asked. 'Where's Mitzi?'

'Blount gave her to a blackguard shopkeeper, who has taken her off into the country. I won't be able to get her till morning. I am not leaving without her. In fact, I don't know how we are to leave at all. Blount is not coming any further on the trip.'

'What did you say to him?' she demanded in an accusing way.

'I told him if he does not like my dog, he can go away.'

'Went into one of your fine rants, did you? You've done a good job of landing us in the suds this time. Lost your diamond necklace, given Sir Edmund, who is a *very eligible gentleman*, a disgust of you and got us stranded in this dump of a place with very little money.'

'We have enough to take the stage to Fareham.'

'Aye, to land ourselves at Weston's doorstep without the diamonds, which are our reason for going, and which he stole in the first place.'

'He won't be much surprised if we don't have them then, will he?' I asked curtly. Maisie is becoming very short-tempered lately, since old Beattie offered for me.

'*I* think you should run along to Sir Edmund's room and make it up with him.'

'He is not in his room, and I would not go if he were.'

'Where is he?'

'Downstairs, probably inquiring for the light-skirt's room, or trying if he can find her sitting in a corner, rolling her eyes at prospective customers. How should *I* know?'

'That coarse, vulgar talk is very unbecoming, Lizzie. Edmund's eyes very nearly left his head today when you called yourself a bitch.'

'I did nothing of the sort. He was hoping she'd jump down from the perch then, when he *insisted* on making her drive out in the cold wind, and she soaking wet. If she doesn't catch pneumonia I'll be much surprised.'

'Too bad if she don't, nasty-tempered animal. Seems a shame to lose out on such an excellent *parti* as Edmund . . .'

'He is not an excellent *parti*. He hates women – *ladies* that is,' I corrected. 'He is fond enough of the other sort.'

'He was asking all kinds of questions about you, Lizzie, any time I was alone with him for a minute. I think he's interested in you.'

'He loathes me, and so do I hate him. Pray tell him so if he asks any more questions. What sort of thing was he asking?'

'He asked if you are always so high-spirited, and just mentioning casually whether you had many beaux and so on. The very kind of question he would ask if he liked you. So have we seen the last of him?'

'Yes, he does not continue with us.'

'Is it definitely settled?'

'I *told* you so, didn't I?'

She looked dissatisfied. She sat biting her lips for three or four minutes, then spoke up. 'He's got the paste neck-lace, Lizzie.'

I knew it was no more than an excuse to get me to call on him. 'He paid for it. He's welcome to it. I suppose he will leave it at the desk for us when he departs.'

'He'll never go without saying goodbye to us.'

'I do not expect to see him again.'

'*One* of us has to thank him for all his outstanding kind-ness – doing so much more than he *had* to. I'm sure he only did it for you, Lizzie, as an excuse to hang around and get to know you better.'

'He knows me pretty well now.'

'I'll have to drag my poor pulsating limb down the hall then,' she began in a weary way, half rising from her chair.

'No, Maisie, you think if you make enough fuss about it, *I* will go down the hall, but I won't, so you might as well sit and pulsate in peace.'

She grumbled on for several minutes, while I interrupted from time to time to mention that poor Mitzi had not even had her dinner. If that wretched Reuben fed her anything, it would be wine. I suggested we retire, but my aunt had a trump up her sleeve.

'I won't be able to sleep a wink, all up in the air as we are. Till I learn whether we are to go alone on the stage tomorrow. . . . And he might forget to leave off the paste necklace, you know, Lizzie.'

I thought he would remember it in the morning, if not before. In fact, I did not see how he could have forgotten it for so long, jingling right in his pocket as it was. One would think a *gentleman* would bring it to us, and apologize while he was about it. I delayed making my preparations for bed, on the watch for an apologetic tap at the door. There was none. At length, Maisie's whining got on my nerves to such an extent I agreed to tap at Sir Edmund's door, before she harangued me, too, into insomnia. I would just ask him if he meant to leave the necklace with me, or keep it. It was a paltry excuse to be sure, but it was not my only one. I also wished to thank him for his attempts at help, and to say goodbye. Because *he* chose to act as a savage was no reason we must behave as badly.

I took a deep breath, screwed up my courage and went out the door.

CHAPTER 7

I was half relieved when there was no reply to my knock. He was having a few glasses of ale before coming upstairs. He might even drink himself into a good enough mood to come to us to apologize. I raised my knuckles to give a second tap, ready to turn and walk away if he did not respond immediately. A scuffling sound within alerted me he was there. He called something – 'bring it in,' it sounded like, which made me think he had ordered wine sent to his room. It also darted into my head he meant to bring it along to share with Maisie and myself. A bottle of wine would form a decent excuse to cover any little embarrassment he might feel. I was close to being in charity with the man, to find him so biddable. I prepared a bright smile in reward.

I hesitated to go in, for a gentleman will sometimes ask a male servant to enter when he is not quite prepared for a young lady's company. I knocked again.

'Come in,' he called, his voice taking on its customary impatience.

I opened the door wide and walked all unsuspecting into a scene of debauchery. He had his jacket and boots off and, while I did not see the trollop from downstairs, I saw a corner of black skirt sticking out from behind the clothes-press. I could not discover whether it hung on a chair or her back, but I could see well enough of a pair of dainty black patent slippers kicked off in the middle of the floor, lending a wildly abandoned air to the place. The wine had already arrived. It awaited their pleasure on a side table.

I was so interested in all this evidence of wantonness that I neglected to look at his face for a few seconds. When I looked up from the black slippers, where my eyes kept returning, I saw him glaring at me with the frustrated look of a baited animal. The lines between nose and mouth were etched deep, the lips clenched so hard the cords in his neck stood out. They were visible right down to his clavicle, for he had his cravat off and his collar open. I was vastly relieved I had not come two minutes later, or God knows what I might have witnessed.

Sir Edmund was speechless. He just glared, mute as a rabbit, but not nearly so timid-looking. I could think of no words to suit the peculiar situation myself. I looked, then heard a shrill laugh come out of my mouth. Horrified, I raised my fingers to try to hold it in. Without making a coherent sound, I turned and fled down the hallway to the safety of Maisie's room. I was laughing so hard by the time I got inside, she could not understand what ailed me.

'What happened?' she kept asking, two or thre times. I had to have a glass of water before I wa sufficiently recovered to tell her.

'He had a woman in his room – undressed!'

That caused her to open up her eyes. 'Glory be to God, you don't mean it!'

'Indeed I do.'

'He'll be so ashamed he'll not show his face to us again.'

'Not to worry, Aunt. I have no thought *now* of letting him off without thanking him most ceremoniously for all his help. I shall ask too whether he still has the necklace, or if he has given it to someone.'

'You're chirping merry now, I see.'

'As merry as a grig in June. The great misogamist, Sir Edmund Blount, caught barefooted with a lightskirt, after all his fine talk of hating women.'

'He never said he hated women, only marriage. Any man enjoys an occasional frolic – especially a bachelor.'

'You have become very lenient in your morality, Aunt. Next you will be telling me you approve of it.'

'If he must cut up a lark, he is wise to do it away from home. I do approve of *that*, at least.'

'What *I* would like to know is when he arranged the details of it. Good gracious, he hadn't more than a few seconds alone with her. He must be quick. But it was likely done when he went downstairs after I gave him a good tongue-lashing. Well, Aunt, I am very much afraid you are going to have a sleepless night. We will get nothing settled with him till morning. I wonder if they stay the whole night, these women.'

'It is not proper for you to conjecture on such matters, Lizzie.'

'That elastic morality of yours has snapped back into

place, I *see.*'

There was a sharp knocking at the door. 'Did you order anything?' I asked her.

'No, nothing.'

I opened the door to see Sir Edmund standing there with his jacket thrown on, not buttoned, and a cravat very much awry. He had taken time to pull on his boots. 'May I come in?' he asked, then barged past me without awaiting an answer.

I peeked my head out the door to glance down the hall. 'You are alone?' I asked pointedly.

'As you see,' he replied, trying to sound offhand. He turned to Maisie, ignoring me. 'How does the ankle go on, Maisie? Not too painful, I hope?'

'The swelling has started to go out of it,' she admitted, happy to avoid the subject she knew I wished to raise. 'I'll be ready to hit the road again by morning. Lizzie tells me you are leaving us.'

'Certainly not! Where did she get that idea?' he asked, assuming a pose of astonishment.

'You expressed the intention of not sharing a carriage with my dog,' I reminded him, while more interesting phrases churned round inside my head. His wary regard told me he was well aware of it.

'No, no. I was joking, of course. I thought you knew it.'

'No, Sir Edmund, I never look for a joke from you.'

'I have *every* intention of going to Fareham. I came to ask at what hour you would like to leave in the morning.'

'You need not have interrupted your – business? – only for that,' I told him. 'We have no notion of leaving before dawn, or anything of the sort.'

'I was not busy,' he said, in a flat, bored voice.

'Then I expect you are very eager to return to your room to *get* busy. Pray do not let us detain you. Eight, shall we say? Or perhaps a later hour would suit you better. . . .' I suggested helpfully.

'Eight is fine. Let us meet for breakfast at eight down-stairs.'

'Agreed. We shall let you go now,' I said, taking his elbow to pilot him to the door. He shook me off.

'I thought a glass of wine might help your aunt sleep more comfortably,' he said.

'I was just thinking the same thing,' Maisie answered.

'I shall order us some, Aunt. Sir Edmund has company. He will not like to keep his guest waiting.'

'There is no one in my room,' he said, looking off toward the window, to avoid looking at me. I did not refute the statement verbally, but only looked all my disbelief at him. 'The person you saw just stepped in in passing, to see if I had had any luck in finding Greenie.'

'She reads minds, does she, that she knew you were looking for him?'

'I mentioned it to her earlier,' he said quickly, then remembered, I believe, having told me he had not time to ask her. 'I mean – later. Not the first time I spoke to her.'

'Ah, yes, that would be about two minutes before she popped in to see if you had found him yet.'

Having no reply, he ignored it. 'I had ordered wine, and meant to offer her a glass. I mistook you for a servant when you knocked. You should not have rushed off so precipitately, Miss Braden. My guest took the idea you did not wish for her acquaintance.'

'She was correct. A gentleman does not customarily introduce *ladies* to such females as your guest, if I am not mistaken.'

'You judge severely. There was nothing amiss with the girl that I could see.'

'Indeed? I should take it sadly amiss if any chance caller of mine, a virtual stranger of the opposite sex, decided to cast off his clothing in my chamber, but then I am old-fashioned.'

Another knock sounded at the door. I was seized with a wild hope the hussy had come after him, but it was a servant with wine. The only manner in which the order could have been given was through the hussy. Sir Edmund had not time to have pounced downstairs and ordered it himself. It served to divert the conversation to wine, then to the necklace and our plans for the morrow.

'I have been giving a good deal of thought to how we should proceed,' he said in a businesslike way.

'When did you have time?' I asked. Both Maisie and he glared.

'After I left you. I thought it might be interesting if we go to Weston Braden's place and say nothing of the missing necklace. Your aunt thinks he might be involved in this imbroglio, Miss Braden. *I* think he is involved in it. I suggest we go and present him with the diamond necklace copy, and say nothing about any theft.'

'A single glance will tell him it is a copy,' I pointed out.

'Not if genuine diamonds have been placed in the

settings. It is the stones that give it away. The metal work is well enough.'

'Have I missed something here? Has someone found the diamonds, or where are we to get these substitutes?'

'From a diamond merchant,' he answered blandly. 'One who deals in old stones. The cut was different in those old days. Bartlett, in Winchester here, is as good a man as we will find outside of London. He won't have just the proper sizes and shapes, of course, but if he can stick in real gems of some sort, we can present it to Weston Braden without blushing.'

'I don't see the point of it,' Maisie said. No more did I. It sounded perfectly ludicrous.

'My thinking is this; if we just present him the copy, he glances at it and says it is obviously a fake. But if we give him a necklace with genuine diamonds in it, he is going to begin to wonder just what it is Greenie stole for him. He will want to check it out, compare them at least.'

'I still don't see the point,' Maisie said.

'You mean we should follow him when he goes to make this comparison, to find out where he has got mine hidden?' I asked.

'Something of the sort. If we are there, we can snoop around and look for it at least. He can hardly claim what you present to him is a fake when it contains real diamonds, unless he is willing to say how he knows. Even to see his face when you give it to him would tell us something. Unless the man is a professional actor, some traces of guilt will be in evidence.'

'He is right, Maisie. I have just been noticing how difficult it is for a guilty man to try to act natural.'

'A conman's game,' Maisie said, choosing not to under-stand me. Sir Edmund directed a cool, dark eye at me, while he reined in his temper. 'It's worth a try at least,' she ventured. 'What does it cost us?'

'A mere bagatelle! Only the price of a whole set of diamonds,' I answered.

'I shan't *buy* them, just borrow or rent them, with a little something down,' Blount said.

'How long would it take to get this substitution done?' I asked.

'A few hours, perhaps; if Bartlett has any stones he can stick in, the actual work won't take longer. We could be at Fareham before dark. *I* think it is our best bet,' Sir Edmund said, looking from one to the other of us for our reaction.

'It is a great deal of trouble to put you to,' I felt obliged to mention. Really I had never expected this degree of cooperation.

The intriguing thing is that he did not even *look* put upon, as he usually did for far less bother than this scheme entailed. In fact, he looked humble and, when we agreed to the scheme, relieved. I suppose between *my* dog and *his* lightskirt, he was feeling guilty. I disliked to raise the subject of Mitzi when he was being so very helpful, but it weighed on my mind, her being with that drunken old Reuben.

'You look concerned. Do you not care for my plan, ma'am?' he asked, as we began our second glass of wine.

'It is not the plan I am thinking about. It is Mitzi.'

All traces of humility and relief vanished from his countenance. 'I hope you are not implying we ought to go after her tonight? I, for one, have had more-than enough excitement and activity for one day.'

'Poor Mitzi,' I said, drawing a long sigh and gazing forlornly out the window. 'I can almost imagine I hear her, howling and whimpering as Reuben beats her. I know I shan't sleep a wink. But Sir Edmund is fatigued with his busy evening. Do not let us detain you longer, sir.'

He bounced to his feet. 'Good evening, ladies. I hope you both sleep well. I know I mean to. I shan't leave my bed this night.' I silently cocked a brow at him, but managed to suppress my smile. His lips clenched in a tight line and did not open to deliver any further words.

CHAPTER 8

Sir Edmund looked positively hagged when he met us in the parlor at eight next morning. He also looked extremely ashamed of himself, as he greeted us holding Mitzi in the crook of his arm.

'Sir Edmund! You got her back! How – when?' I was overcome with emotion. I held my arms out to receive her, but she turned her head, looked up, and licked Sir Edmund's chin lovingly, showing no inclination to come to me. She, who had always had an instinctive dislike of men. I often thought it was why Beattie gave her to me, because she held him in such contempt.

'Last night,' he said casually, as though he had done no more than walk to the door and whistle for her.

'Did she run away from Reuben?'

'Lord no, I had to go all the . . . I drove out and picked her up.'

'Edmund! I didn't *really* mean for you to do that.'

'I had nothing else to do,' he made a point of telling me.

'So much trouble. Thank you.' I gave him my prettiest

smile in gratitude, then tried once more to retrieve my dog. She clung with her nails tenaciously to his sleeve, crouching back in the crook of his elbow.

'You shouldn't have let her bearlead you into so much trouble,' Maisie scolded.

'What have you done to her? How did you bring her round your thumb? She does not usually take to men,' I said, still having no luck to get her into my arms.

'We have reached a mutually satisfactory arrangement. She don't bite me, and I don't kick her.' As he spoke, he massaged her neck with gentle strokes of the fingers. No doubt he had seen me lull her by the same means, and was quick-witted enough to have noticed it. He put her on the floor, where she capered happily about his boots, still spurning my advances.

When breakfast came, I offered her bits of bacon to try to lure her from his chair. She lifted her nose and looked disdainfully down it at me and my poor bribes. 'Are you not eating this morning, Sir Edmund?' I asked him.

'We have had breakfast already, Mitzi and I, and our morning constitutional. As soon as you ladies have finished eating, we shall go to Bartlett and see what he can do for us. Will you tackle the trip, Maisie?'

'I'll not undertake any unnecessary walking yet. I'll sit quietly here in the parlor with the newspapers. Just pamper myself.'

'I bet you are not pampered at home,' he replied, which set her smiling at me.

'Having alienated my dog's affections, are you now starting on my aunt's?' I demanded.

'That's it. I figure two out of three conquests is the best I can hope for.'

When we had finished eating, we rose to go. My pug frisked at Blount's heels, hinting to be carried. 'You stay with Maisie,' I ordered.

'I don't mind if she tags along,' Edmund offered. I was so angry with my pet that I shoved her inside the door and closed it. I received a wounded look from my companion for my trouble.

'Did you get to bed at all last night?' I asked him, for I really felt some extraordinary consideration due him for getting Mitzi back.

'Don't start carping on *that* again, Lizzie,' he said angrily.

'*What?*'

'All right, I confess. You caught me with a woman of pleasure in my room. You know I am a bachelor. My doings are public knowledge at Woldwood, where I live. I enjoy a good reputation. Occasionally, when I am out of town. . . .'

'Sir Edmund, I didn't mean *that*! I was only worried your going after Mitzi had kept you up most of the night. You don't have to apologize to *me* for – for anything. It is none of my concern. I was only teasing you last night.'

He was ready to slay himself for having misunderstood and confessed. He looked remarkably like a little boy who has inadvertently admitted his sins when he was not even suspected. 'I misunderstood the nature of your question. You expressed such rampant interest in the matter last night. . . .'

'Not interest, only surprise. Pray, let us change the subject. *Did* you get any sleep?'

'Demmed little. The mutt woke me before six.'

I could not resist. It was utterly unworthy, but my next question was, '*Did* you complete your transaction with the lightskirt?'

'Bartlett's shop is this way,' he said, taking my elbow and turning me round a corner. 'We'll walk. It is not far. No, I didn't, if you really care.'

I had thought he meant to ignore my question, had taken offense at it. I looked up to see him smiling down at me in the strangest way. It was an *intimate* smile. Significant, and very attractive. He could be a handsome man, if only he would let off scowling occasionally. 'Mind you must keep a *very* sharp eye on me, Lizzie. I am inclined to stray when I am away from home.'

'You may not have succeeded with the woman, but you had good luck with Mitzi. How did you win her?'

'We share a common taste, beefsteak. And about the woman, it was by no means a lack of *success*, only of opportunity, when you came barging in. I have been thinking about this trip to Braden's place, Lizzie,' he said, changing the subject. 'Rusholme, is it?'

'Yes, near Fareham. What about it?'

'He will find it peculiar that you drag me along, a stranger. How is my presence to be explained?'

'I'll tell him about the accident, that my carriage is wrecked, without mentioning the theft. Tell him you are delivering me.'

'That will incline him to think I should leave as soon as

you are safely delivered, will it not? I plan to stick around. You'll have to come up with something else.'

'I cannot call you a relative. He knows all my kin. It would not look natural to invite a casual friend either.'

'I could become your fiancé for the duration of the visit.'

'That would make a decent excuse for your presence, but should we not give you a new name? You would not want word to get about the countryside the elusive Sir Edmund Blount is engaged. A man in your position – there might be someone there who knows you.'

'No one who knows me would believe it,' he answered. 'It is rather your fair name we must think of. Would the rumor be likely to run back to Westgate?'

'Not at all. The only connection Weston has there is us. Neither Maisie nor I would tell anyone, of course.'

'There we are then. Miss Braden, would you do me the honor to be my fiancée for a day or two, on the strict understanding that we are never to get married?'

'Lawdamercy, Sir Edmund! How you do sweet-talk a lady! How can I resist? I will be happy to be your unintended wife, but for an absolute maximum of forty-eight hours.'

'Agreed.'

The ensuing conversation was so foolish it is not worth committing to paper. I was shocked to find Blount capable of foolishness. The nonsense continued till we reached Mr Bartlett's workshop. The jeweler was a man with an oval head, fringed in white. He wore tiny glasses that rested on the tip of his nose. He was puzzled at the nature of our request-to put real diamonds into a cheap setting. He insisted he had not any of the proper size or shape. He had had doings with Sir Edmund's family before, however, and was not loath to do what he could for him. The necklace was left with him, the understanding being that he would do his best, but he explained that the job would take longer than a few hours. No amount of urging from Sir Edmund, or bald assertions that it wouldn't take a minute to pry out the glass and just stick in proper stones, changed his opinion.

'Come back at three,' he said. When Sir Edmund mentioned two, Bartlett changed it to three-thirty.

I got Sir Edmund out the door before the hour could be pushed any further forward.

'Let us go and see how Maisie and Mitzi get on,' I suggested.

'You are not the type of lady I usually get unengaged to,' he told me, shaking his head sadly. 'Feather-headed. Are we to go to your uncle without an engagement ring?'

'It cannot be worth buying one for two days. With your philosophy, I cannot think it will have any other use.'

'It will not be a total loss. I can give it to Wilma.'

'Who is Wilma?' I asked. I immediately wished I had not, for I had a sudden feeling she was a sultry-eyed female with raven curls.

'She is poor Willie's fiancée. Wife now. My brother was married yesterday, remember?'

'Surely Willie bought her an engagement ring himself?'

She wouldn't mind having two, he thought.

'You are careless with your money. Let us pick up a tin one at the everything store. It won't turn green for a few days. Uncle Weston will hardly examine it through a magnifying glass. A sham ring for a sham engagement.'

'Good thinking.'

We entered the first store of the proper sort we came to. They had a fine selection of trinkets. 'I want to buy me fiancée an engagement ring,' Sir Edmund said, causing the proprietor to examine us closely.

'I don't sell jewelry,' the man answered.

'Nonsense, of course you do. What are all these things here?' Blount ran his eye over an assortment of garish red glass beads, pins and tin rings.

'This is servants' toy stuff,' the man replied, frowning at us. He checked me out thoroughly to be sure I was not a servant being conned by a dandy.

'That is exactly what we want. Here, try this one, Lizzie,' he said, lifting up a narrow band, painted with some metallic stuff that was more coppery than gold in hue.

I put out my left hand for him to slide the tin on the third finger. It spun around loosely. It was so cheap Sir Edmund bent it as he lifted it from the finger back to the man. It squeezed into an oval at the slightest exertion of the fingers. 'This one is for ten minute engagements,' he told me. 'Find us something that won't lose its shape or shine for a couple of days,' he said to the clerk.

The man rooted behind the counter to produce a higher quality of trinket. 'These cost a shilling,' he cautioned.

'An expensive business,' Edmund repined, shaking his head dismally. He lifted one out and tried it. It fit well enough, but looked so very like the other that it would not pass even a cursory examination.

'Have you got anything embossed, maybe some leaves or something to hide the glare of the tin?' Edmund asked. 'I'll be getting into deep financial waters here,' he said aside to me. 'We're talking a crown at least.'

'You're a shrewd judge of value,' the clerk praised him, rummaging for a piece yet more elaborate than the last.

'This is more like it! What more could a girl ask?' I exclaimed when my ring was handed to me. 'From a yard away, it would fool the most suspicious. What do you think, Edmund?'

'Plenty good enough for you. Stick it on,' he answered.

With the embossed circle of tin on my finger, we left the shop, while the man within shook his head in confusion at the way of gentry folk.

Sir Edmund's manner of revealing our plan to Maisie that he pose as my fiancé was to say baldly to her, as soon as we entered her room, 'You must congratulate us, Maisie. We are engaged. Show her your ring, Lizzie.'

I can only assume my aunt was suffering some mental disorder after her accident the day before. She believed him! Worse, she let out a whoop of delight at my conquest. She started up from her chair and came limping forward, wearing a smile as wide as her face. 'I knew it!' she shrieked, laughing inanely. 'I could tell from the way you were carrying on last night, Lizzie, that you loved him! Why else would you have been so upset about that. . . .' She was too nice to continue. 'Oh Edmund, I couldn't be happier! What a wonderful match for my niece.'

'Thank you, Maisie. We have your approval then?' he

asked, sliding his demmed dark eyes over to laugh at me.

'Have you taken leave of your senses, Maisie?' I asked sharply. 'Sir Edmund is joking. We have decided to tell Weston we are engaged, to give Edmund an excuse to accompany us.'

'But the ring!' she exclaimed, staring at it.

'Tin, to add an air of authenticity to the masquerade,' I told her.

She laughed then as though it were a marvelous joke. 'I *did* think it sudden, to be sure. Only twenty-four hours. It usually takes a little longer than that.'

'How long does it *usually* take her?' he asked.

'Ha, she is slow as molasses in January. She never had but the one offer from old Beattie, and *that* took twenty-five years.'

'I have so had offers! Both the ministers. . . . Oh, never mind.'

'That's right. I forgot Reverend Cox and Doctor Leiterman, but clerics, you know. They would not suit Lizzie. She is too lively for that.'

'She'll have me worn to a thread before our two-day engagement is over. Bartlett will have the necklace ready by three.'

'Three-thirty,' I corrected.

'I'll go over and start pestering him an hour before that. Well, ladies, we have a couple of hours before luncheon. What would you like to do? Why don't I take you out for a drive, Maisie? You must be bored to fidgets, sitting here watching that mutt all day long.' The mutt, meanwhile, was pawing at his trousers, hinting to be taken up.

'It sounds good,' she answered at once. 'Where shall we go?'

'In Winchester, one does one's duty and goes to the cathedral,' he informed her, 'unless, of course, one has the excellent excuse of a sprained ankle, in which case she and her escort are excused.'

We were deprived of a visit to the famous cathedral, which I would very well like to have seen, and so would Maisie, though she is shy of putting her wishes forward. Blount hired a team at a stable to keep the borrowed grays fresh for the dash to Fareham. Some friend of his had a dairy farm north of Winchester. That was our outing – to go and look at very much the sort of thing we have to see every day. With Maisie's bad ankle, she sat on the verandah with the farmer's wife, Mrs. Langton, while I was dragged through barns and pastures, being told by Edmund that what I was seeing was extremely interesting to me, as I too was in the business. I did not trouble to tell him we left all that work in Berrigan's hands.

The Langtons gave us luncheon. As I found the roast beef quite delicious, I should imagine Edmund gagged on every bite, but he was too polite to say so when he was not paying for his meal, as he did at an inn. We had to hasten through our meal to get back to Winchester in time to visit Bartlett an hour before the necklace was ready. The only one of us outside of Blount who enjoyed the morning was Mitzi. She was well amused pestering Langton's cattle. She was through with me entirely. Blount was her new master. She seldom left his heels.

Shortly after three-thirty we were back with the necklace. It did not look exactly like my own, but it looked better than it had. Some of the stones were of the wrong size and shape, but they were at least diamonds, and diamonds of an old cut. Nestled in its proper box with the Elizabethan plaque, it would have fooled any but an expert, which Uncle Weston, unfortunately, was.

CHAPTER 9

$\mathcal{I}$t was a short trip to Rusholme, about sixteen miles. The team of grays borrowed from Edmund's friend made it without baiting. We arrived just in time for dinner, at six. Uncle Weston had about given up on seeing us. I had mentioned we would arrive around noon. Weston Braden, I happen to know, is sixty-five, but he looks older. He is a rumpled anachronism of a man that no valet can keep presentable. His hair is white, worn in the old style – longish, pulled into a tail behind. He has no pretensions to fashion. As often as not he wears an old fustian coat about his place, but in honor of our visit he was rigged out in a blue one. He is somewhat stout, ruddy-complexioned, with bright hazel eyes. Gout necessitates his hobbling along with a walking stick. He is out of style with the world at large, but in the doorway of his half-timbered Elizabethan home, he looks just right – a portly, sixteenth-century English squire. One expects to hear a 'forsooth' or 'sirrah' when he opens his mouth.

I introduced Sir Edmund as my fiancé, never thinking I

would have to do more than make the statement. I was in grave error. Weston took an inordinate interest in the matter.

'Why, you never mentioned a word of being engaged, Lizzie!' he exclaimed, greatly surprised.

'It happened only recently, Uncle.'

'Isn't that nice. I had despaired of ever seeing you settled. So you are Lizzie's young man,' he continued, shaking Blount's hand.

'I have that honor,' Edmund confessed, unblushing.

'Blount. Blount – the name sounds familiar,' Uncle said next. 'You wouldn't be the Blount who owns Woldwood, where the fine cattle are bred?'

'I have that honor, too,' Blount answered modestly.

'Well, now, isn't that fine.' Weston smiled fondly at first me, then my catch. 'You have done well for yourself, missie. Very well indeed. She is sly as a fox, Sir Edmund. She has kept mum as a mole about the whole thing.'

'Very likely she is ashamed of me,' Edmund replied, with a disparaging smile.

This was treated as humor of a high order. After he had finished laughing, Weston asked, 'How do things go on at Westgate? Not too prosperously I fear, as you are ready to sell me the necklace.'

'Not prosperously at all, Uncle. That Berrigan fellow you saddled us with is a disaster.'

'Is he indeed? I am surprised to hear it. He came highly recommended. I'll look about and find someone else for you. Or perhaps Sir Edmund would be interested. . . .' His relief at being rid of us was genuine.

Once I was there, actually facing my uncle, I knew perfectly well it was nonsense to think he had anything to do with Greenie or the stolen jewelry. I believe Sir Edmund was thinking the same thing. He observed Weston closely, then a sort of puzzled frown settled on his harsh features as he glanced to me.

Maisie came forward to make her greeting and be welcomed. When she was seen to be carrying a walking stick, Weston thought he had a fellow-sufferer in gout. 'No, I had an accident,' she told him. 'Our carriage was over-turned just outside of Devizes. Lizzie is wearing a patch, you must have noticed.'

'How did it happen?' he inquired.

'One of those demmed Corinthians was hunting the squirrel, and capsized us,' Edmund explained, in well-feigned vexation.

'They ought to be whipped at the cart's tail, every one of them,' Weston said in a supporting way. 'Well, come in and let us have some refreshment. You ladies will want to change for dinner.'

The difficulty in this scheme was explained. 'Our trunks ought to be here by tomorrow,' Edmund said. 'I sent word to Devizes to forward them here. I forgot to mention it to you, Lizzie. I did it this morning, when I was up early with Mitzi.'

'Good, I am happy to hear it.' I hoped it was true, and not more invention from my fellow actor.

'No matter. We are not at all grand here, in the country,' Uncle told us, relieved to be spared the bother of dressing himself.

We had a glass of wine while dinner was given its final preparation. 'I am most eager to see the necklace,' Uncle said. 'Do you have it in your reticule, Lizzie, that I might have a look now, while we await dinner?'

'Edmund is carrying it,' I told him.

I knew it was in Edmund's pocket, but he did not produce it. Perhaps he was afraid my uncle would get to compare it to the other while we were washing up for dinner. 'I'll get it later,' he said.

There was nothing amiss in the meal. Uncle sets a good table, but the conversation was uneasy. The matter of my wedding arose again. Weston expressed a natural interest in its date. 'When do you plan to tie the knot?' he asked.

'Pretty soon,' Edmund answered, while I simultaneously said, 'Not for a while yet.' Our eyes flew to each other to exchange a guilty look at this blunder.

'The date is not settled,' Maisie explained, easing us out of the touchy situation.

We spoke of my brother, of Weston's stepson Glandower. 'Who will run Westgate after the wedding?' Weston asked. 'Jeremy never took any interest in it. You will want a good steward.'

'I will be taking care of those details,' Edmund replied. 'It is the problem of leaving Westgate untenanted that causes the delay in our wedding.'

'Will you go to Woldwood with them, Maisie?' he asked next.

Again we came a cropper. Her 'no' collided solidly with my 'oh, yes' and Edmund's 'certainly she will.'

Uncle looked at us, bewildered. 'That is not quite settled

either,' Maisie told him. 'They want me to go, but I feel I ought to stay home to look after Jeremy when he comes home, you know.'

'You will be much better off with us,' Edmund scolded in a proprietary way. 'Lizzie agrees with me.'

'Yes, for Jeremy is so seldom home you would be lonesome, Aunt,' I added, doing my bit to bolster the illusion of an approaching wedding. I realized the farce was becoming more complicated than I had ever anticipated.

Edmund diverted the conversation to farming, which got us through dessert without utter disaster. Uncle was eager enough to see the diamonds that he kept Edmund behind for only one small glass of port. Ten minutes after we left the gentlemen, they joined us in the saloon.

'Shall we have a look at it now?' Uncle asked, rubbing his hands together in delighted anticipation.

'Why not? Here it is,' Edmund said, sliding his hand into his inner jacket pocket to extract the green case.

We three visitors risked one curious, swift exchange of a look while Uncle took the box, then we all stared hard at him, ready to discover any flaw in his expression, any sign indicating guilt.' He opened the lid, nodding and smiling innocently at the plaque inside. Then his gaze went to the necklace, still smiling, still innocent. Within two seconds, some little frown formed between his white brows. He picked the jewelry up, looked closely at it for a while longer, then looked at me.

'It looks different somehow,' he said. 'These matching stones here, third from the center, are oval – I made sure they were done in the rounder style.'

'You must be mistaken,' I answered, trying for a noncha-lant air.

'I must be,' he agreed reluctantly. 'This is very strange. The center stone is larger than I recall, and some of the others smaller.'

'You have not seen it for a long while,' I mentioned.

'True, but I have the replica, you recall, that I often take a look at. I had it out after I received your letter, Lizzie. I had thought it was a perfect copy, but I was mistaken.'

We three conspirators risked another quick glance, noting he had voluntarily mentioned the replica. 'Why do you not get the copy, and compare them?' Edmund asked. His speech sounded so extremely significant to me I was sure Uncle would demand at once what chicanery we were up to.

'Yes, I'll do that,' was all he said.

When he turned to leave the room, still carrying the necklace, Edmund followed at his heels. They went no farther than a few yards down the hall to the study. When they returned, Uncle carried his copy in the other hand.

He laid the pair on the table under a lamp, while the four of us gathered round to stare at them. Uncle's copy looked better than ours, despite the paste stones. The design was more pleasing, the size and shape of the 'stones' better matched.

'Lizzie, you wretch, confess!' Uncle said, lifting his blue eyes to examine me critically.

'Wh-what do you mean?' I asked, my voice trembling.

'I don't understand your remark, Mr Braden,' Edmund said quickly, hotly, like any lover defending his fiancée.

Uncle shook his head sadly. 'You have *tampered* with this, Liz. Had some of the stones pried out and sold, then replaced them with others that do not suit so well. It is no longer a genuine antique. Oh, I can see the stones are old, the style of the faceting is certainly correct, but the actual stones are not the originals. Unless you. can tell me where I might find the ones that ought to be in it, I am not sure I want to buy it.'

'Bartlett, in Winchester, took a look at this on our way through, Mr Braden. He certainly said nothing about any of the stones not being genuine,' Edmund told him, still feigning offense on my behalf.

'They are genuine diamonds; they are genuinely *old* diamonds, but they are not the diamonds Queen Elizabeth gave to Sir Eldridge. Well, some of them undoubtedly are. Those at the back on either side look very much as they ought.' As he spoke, he pulled a jeweler's loupe from his trousers pocket and put it to his eye, lifting up the necklace to scrutinize it.

'They have not been put in any too carefully either,' he added, picking at some of the mountings. 'Pity,' he said, shaking his head at our botched piece. His interest in the stones was strong enough that he did not take a close look at the metal, which would have told him, perhaps, exactly what he held.

'Why did you do it?' Weston asked me.

'Let us first confirm that she *did* do it,' Edmund objected.

The ball was in my hands. Was I to confess, or not? I looked to Edmund for a clue. 'I daresay it happened after that spot of trouble about your infected cattle, when you were short of funds,' he prompted, giving me the clue I was to confess.

'Yes, that is when I did it.'

'Now, Lizzie, that was very wrong of you, to try to sell me the thing in such a condition,' Weston said. 'Unethical, I believe is not too strong a word. I am disappointed in you.'

'She hadn't much choice, with Berrigan decimating the herd on her!' Edmund shot back angrily, with an accusing stare at Braden, the supplier of poor stewards, and a protective hand on my arm. 'He is *right*, however. It was wrong of you to do it, Lizzie. You should have told me.'

'Ladies don't understand these matters,' Braden said, taking his turn at exculpating and forgiving me. 'I will oftimes come across a wonderful, rare old piece of furniture, where some well-meaning housewife has had good Elizabethan brocade ripped off a chair, to be replaced with new. Authenticity means nothing to them.'

'Nine-tenths of them prefer gaudy rubbish, given a choice,' Blount agreed, giving my tin ring a little twirl on my finger.

'Where did you sell them?' Weston asked. His next speech would be to inquire whether they were retrievable. I was sinking, sinking into a morass from which I saw no extrication.

'Different times, at different places,' I replied vaguely.

'Local merchants, I daresay? There will be no tracing them,' Weston said sadly. I encouraged him to continue in this illusion, to muddy the waters as much as possible. The whole trip was futile: Uncle knew nothing about the theft.

After a few moments regretting and repining, the subject was dropped. 'Are you interested in antiques at all, Sir Edmund?' Uncle asked hopefully.

Edmund was willing to divert the talk to harmless matters till we had got together to discuss our next step. He confessed, or pretended, to some interest in archaic things to pass the next hour. Maisie and I had already admired his walls, feet thick, his mottled glass window panes, his badly carved furnishings and misshapen dishes and flatware. It was Edmund's turn. He was led from room to room, inventing praise, while my aunt and I passed a more comfortable evening resting, drinking tea and making plans.

'We'll have to meet with Edmund tonight after Uncle retires,' I said. 'We shall get away from here as soon as possible tomorrow.'

'Right after our trunks arrive,' Maisie added. 'My gown got up on its own and closed the window at the inn last night, it is so soiled.'

Later the gentlemen returned, had tea, and then it was time for bed, though the hour was not at all advanced. 'Sleep in if you like in the morning,' Uncle offered. 'I breakfast at seven, but I am old-fashioned. Goodnight to you all. I'll take you along to your rooms, to save disturbing Mrs. Welter.'

No lights were left burning below. We went perforce with Uncle upstairs, with nothing settled as to when we might meet again for a private chat. Maisie was shown to her room first, myself next. 'I've put you in the west wing, next to myself,' I heard Uncle tell Edmund as they retreated down the hall.

As their doors closed behind them, Maisie's opened. 'What are we to do now?' she asked.

'I shall leave my door open a while. I expect to see Edmund peep his head out any moment.'

'Excellent. I'll let you two decide what is to be done. You had better meet with him *downstairs*, Lizzie,' she added, with a nod of her head.

'Let us all meet in *your* room, if it is only the proprieties that trouble you.'

'Oh, I think it would be better if the two of you met alone,' she said, with a little laugh.

'Setting up your shingle as a matchmaker, Maisie?'

'I just want to get you out of Westgate, so I can have a clear field with old Beattie,' she answered.

Of course she joked, but that *old* look had left her since our trip's beginning. The excitement was good for her. Even with her ankle bothering her, she was looking younger, happier. She closed the door softly. I stood alone, waiting.

CHAPTER 10

I had a long wait. For close to ten minutes I stood, wondering whether I ought to slip down the hallway and tap gently on Edmund's door. Just as I took the decision to do it, his door opened and he came out. He had left his boots behind to tread more softly. He had also sprinkled himself with scent. He carried no candle or lamp. I had an inkling he might suggest we two meet without Maisie's chaperonage, and waited with some amusement to see if I was correct.

'There is no point in disturbing Maisie. We'll slip downstairs,' were the first words that left his mouth. He took my hand, while I quickly lifted up my lamp in the other to slip quietly along to the stairs. Like a pair of thieves in the night, we descended, trying to avoid the more loudly protesting steps.

'In here,' he said, when we reached the landing. We went back into the saloon recently deserted. I put down my lamp, then we went to the sofa.

'You could have knocked me over with a feather when

he brought out his copy,' Edmund said. I will not say I was disappointed exactly at the businesslike speech, but to tell the truth, I rather thought the scent and the hand-holding augured a different statement. 'I was sure we had got that copy from Reuben. It *is* a copy. I took the cork-brained idea for a moment he was brass-faced enough to have brought the stolen original out to fool us, but they were paste stones, mounted in good metal. What do you make of this turn?'

'I tried to tell you and Maisie that Uncle had nothing to do with it.'

'Oh, but he had! Who else but he and yourself *could* have done it? Had another copy made, I mean. For that you require either the original or a good copy. You don't suggest someone from around Westgate is behind it? Did Beattie know the reason for your visit?'

'No, he did not even know *about* the visit. He is no felon.'

'I wouldn't trust him an inch beyond my nose, but stealing is not his customary crime.'

'What is?' I asked at once, full of curiosity.

'Pestering women. Can't keep his hands off them. It is the curse of widowers. And bachelors,' he added with a smile, to show he jested, though his hand did in fact reach for my fingers again. I moved beyond his reach, which returned him to the path of business. 'So the copy we bought must have been made from Weston's copy. It looks highly suspicious to me that he would have a second copy made.'

'Maybe someone else did it. We did not ask whether he

has someone resembling our wall-eyed, green-jacketed friend in his employ. The whole could have been done by his servants.'

'Or his grinning stepson. Maisie has no opinion of *him*. I have not heard *your* verdict on the fellow.'

'I don't know him very well. I met him a few times here. He did not come to Westgate with Uncle. He spends most of his time in London since his mother's death. It is not likely he knew of my visit, or its reason.'

'That should be easy to discover. We'll make inquiries tomorrow while we are digging for word on Greenie. Meanwhile, tonight, I plan to go over his study. He had the replica necklace out loose on his desk, but there is an old safe in the corner that might be coaxed into opening for us, if you have a hairpin to spare.'

'What do you hope to find in it? The diamonds?'

'I don't *hope*, exactly. After the amount of trouble we have been put to, I don't plan to walk away without exploring all avenues. You stand guard for me. I'll have a go at the safe now.'

As he finished his speech, there was the unmistakable squawk of the stairs being subjected to a heavy weight. 'Maisie?' Edmund asked in a low voice. I shook my head in a negative.

'Uncle,' I prophesied, with a worried thought to the candle, which would alert him to our presence.

More practically, Edmund grabbed it and extinguished the flame between his thumb and finger, plunging us into darkness, while the steps came closer, hit the landing and advanced hesitantly toward the saloon. 'He saw the light,'

Edmund whispered. His fingers, in the darkness, groped for mine as we turned toward the doorway. A pale orange glow appeared, signaling Uncle's lamp. I never felt so cheap in my life. What would he think, to see us sitting there in the darkness? I knew I would blurt out the whole truth if Weston asked me a single question.

'Who's there?' Uncle called, his voice strained with fear, or suspicion. 'Is it you, Glandower?'

Ever inventive, Edmund put his arms around me and kissed me, with the greatest enthusiasm. I was nonplussed, till I realized why he did so extraordinary a thing. He meant to gammon Uncle we fiancés were indulging in a bout of love-making, to discourage him from other thoughts. I think he might have created the impression without *quite* so long an embrace. It was not the optimum time for me to gauge his expertise, but even in my distracted state I knew he was no amateur. The circle of light came closer, causing me the most acute attack of embarrassment. I pushed Edmund away from me and gasped. No acting was required for me to play the blushing damsel.

'Sorry,' Uncle muttered, feeling much as I did myself to judge by his tone. 'Thought I saw a light burning. I made sure it was Glandower come home.'

'It's only us,' I murmured.

'Sorry if we frightened you,' Edmund added.

'No, no. That's all right. I came down to get some papers from my desk. I can't sleep, so may as well answer a few letters – business letters.' He turned, in a hurry to leave us.

'Since we have been found out, we shall beg a light from

you,' Edmund said, disentangling his arms from me and arising to relight our taper.

I felt we ought to make some mention of going back upstairs, as I had not the nerve to go breaking into Uncle's safe after this episode.

'Thank you, sir,' I heard Edmund say, as calmly as though it were broad daylight, and we had been doing no more than talking together. 'We shall be retiring very soon. Lizzie and I have a few matters to discuss privately. Her aunt is always with us during the day, and we have sunk to a secret tryst to accomplish it.'

'I understand. I was young myself once. Engaged after all, and Lizzie, I know, is to be relied upon to behave with discretion. I shan't disturb you again.'

He left. Edmund returned to the sofa and put an arm around my shoulders, which I promptly removed. 'He might come back,' he pointed out.

'He said he would not.'

Edmund pulled away rather quickly. I took the absurd notion he was going to apologize. 'Don't apologize. I know why you did it,' I said, wishing to terminate any further reference to the love-making.

'*Apologize*? I expected congratulations!'

'That was quick thinking on your part. There, I hope you are satisfied.'

He leaned forward, smiling mischievously. 'I am not satisfied that easily – when I am traveling.'

I remembered very well his propensity to dissipation when away from his home, but was determined not to show it. 'You will not break into the safe tonight, after this?' I asked.

'The perfect time. He has promised not to disturb us again. There – he is going back upstairs.'

We sat listening to the squawks mount higher, reach the top, then go on beyond hearing. 'Let's go,' Edmund said.

We went along to the study where a large, heavy, black vault sat unhidden in the corner. Like most objects in the house, it dated from the age of Elizabeth I. They were good locksmiths in those days. The door even seemed loose – it was possible to jiggle it and see it give slightly, but it was impossible to pry it open with a hairpin, letter opener, clasp knife or any other makeshift device. I was extremely nervous, and kept going to the door to listen for Uncle's return. At length, Edmund conceded defeat.

'I'm going to get one of those things,' he said, glaring at the safe. 'It would take a professional to get it open, and it could not be lifted out of your house with anything less than a crane.'

'Let us go,' I said, my nerves stretched wire thin.

'We'll have a look at his desk while we are here.'

The desk's surface held about two years' correspondence, all in a jumbled welter. My own letter was there, half a dozen from Glandower, some asking for money, some declining or accepting invitations to visit. There were bills and receipts and a brief note from Aunt Vera, my father's sister, giving a highly colored account of my financial difficulties at Westgate, ending with the assertion that if it was beyond poor Lizzie to make a decent match, she ought at least to hint Jeremy towards an heiress. While interesting, neither this letter nor any of the other paper was at all helpful to our quest.

'Let us go,' I suggested two or three times, while Edmund yanked open drawers and rifled quickly through more papers.

Something in the bottom of one had caught his attention. I went to read over his shoulder, but as it was up to my eyes, I had to jiggle him aside and get in front of him. What he held was a stack, not thin either, of IOUs bearing Glandower's name.

'The boy gambles heavily,' he commented, as I mentally tallied up the chits. They came to nearly five thousand pounds, over a period of two years.

'And *loses*! What an expensive fribble he is!'

'I wonder what he finds to *grin* about, with all this bad luck.'

'He doesn't, really. Maisie is jealous because Glandower will get this estate, which she had ear-marked for Jeremy, you see. Let us put them back and go.'

With a last look all around, we left, to return to the saloon and our sofa. 'There is nothing more to be done here,' I said. 'We'll make discreet inquiries tomorrow about Greenie, and to learn whether Glandower was here when I wrote to Uncle about the necklace.'

'And if he wasn't?' Edmund asked.

'If he was not, I must go to Bow Street.'

'And if he *was* here, then we go after him. It strikes me a boy who bilks his stepfather of five thousand pounds would not be above stealing a necklace worth the same sum. Certainly he is not above suspicion in any case.'

'But he is in London,' I pointed out.

'You can get to London from here, Lizzie,' he pointed out.

'But it's so far away, and expensive . . .'

'It won't be that expensive. I have a house we can stay at. As to the astronomical distance of sixty or seventy miles, I expect to have my carriage tomorrow. Our trunks are in it.'

'*More* money wasted. How much has this cost, all told?'

'A not so small fortune, but then you have made me economize in other expensive areas – my old traveling vice I refer to – so we can afford it.'

'Oh, dear, and they'll be even *more* expensive in London – your vices, I mean.'

'That's true. You pay through the nose for your pleasure in the city. *You* have something to look forward to. The colonel was London-bound, was he not?'

'Yes, but I didn't get his address. I had no idea we would end up there.'

'I would like to go to London. I usually go every spring, but missed it this year.'

'Ah, yes, spring is the time for your hobby of chasing lightskirts.'

'Just so.

The cuckoo then, on every tree,
Mocks married men.

It is the season that belongs peculiarly to us bachelors. I find late summer a suitable alternative, however.'

'Take care you don't end up a tenant-for-life, like poor Willie.'

'I keep thinking about Willie.'

'*Poor* Willie, you mean?'

'I am beginning to change my mind about his misfortune,' he said, laying an arm nonchalantly along the back of the sofa, which also put it across my shoulders. 'I have enjoyed being an engaged man.' His other hand reached for the tin ring which proclaimed his status.

'I advise you to dart home to Woldwood as fast as your friend's grays can carry you, Edmund. This trip is going to your head.'

'No, to my heart.' He sat looking at me, and the ring on my finger. Then he raised his eyes, hunched his shoulders and said, very offhandedly, 'I'm willing to risk it.' The arm that rested on the sofa inched lower, till his hand fell on my shoulder. I leaped up, wary of what would come next. 'I assume you are not?' he asked.

'Let us wait and see what we discover tomorrow about Glandower and Greenie.'

'Very well,' he said, in a brusque, offended way. We went upstairs silently together. 'Goodnight,' he said at my door, rather coolly, without even slackening his pace.

'Goodnight,' I answered solemnly.

He looked back over his shoulder, one short, angry glare, but said nothing more.

CHAPTER 11

*M*aisie did not reply to my knock. When I entered her room, the soft sound of snoring told me she was not so keen to hear the 'no news' that she had lost any sleep over it. In the morning, I informed her what had passed.

'My money is on Glandower,' she said, pleased to have her whipping boy as the last remaining suspect.

Uncle Weston had taken his breakfast before us, but came to the table to bear us company. A commanding looked directed to me from Edmund urged me to institute the necessary questions, before ever I had poured cream in my coffee, or hardly said good morning.

After a brief interval, I said, 'Has Glandower been home recently, Uncle?'

'Yes, he comes by often, but doesn't stay as long as I would like. He is always darting off.'

'When was his last visit?' I pressed.

'He was here last week with a friend. A nice young fellow he met in London.'

'I am offended he did not stay to meet me,' I said, to hear positive confirmation he had been here at the proper time to know of my coming.

'He would like to have stayed longer, but as I said, he had a friend with him who had to leave, so Glandower left too. Glan returned to London; his friend went along to meet someone else.'

'Glandower went alone to London?' I asked, wondering how to broach the subject of Greenie.

'Yes, he set out alone, but was to meet his valet along the way. That wall-eyed fellow he has hired lately to look after him. The lad had some business he had to see to at his home. He was to meet Glan somewhere along the way to London. The young fellows nowadays won't be seen in public without their valets to lend them consequence.'

I could feel the tension at the table, though of course none of us commented on these interesting statements – that Glandower knew of my visit and had the felon in his employ.

'Where does he put up in London?' was Edmund's question.

'He has a little cottage on Downing Street, not far from the Prime Minister's residence. I have been to it. He has a nice bit of garden going down to Saint James's Park. I once saw the Prime Minister strolling in the park. Glandower sees all the ministers passing by. It is a very good address.'

'Good for what? Is the boy interested in politics?' Edmund asked.

'Oh, no. An *interesting* spot was all I meant. Glandower

is not keen on politics. He will take over here soon. He is enjoying his last days of freedom, while he is young.'

Maisie bridled up at this speech, but it was for Edmund to issue the verbal insult. 'He is not all that young. It seems to me you could use him now to give you a hand about the place, Mr Braden.'

'So I could,' Uncle admitted sadly.

'We'll call on him while we are in London. I am taking the ladies to town for a bit of shopping. In fact, since you are not interested in buying the necklace at this time, we shall leave today, as soon as my carriage and the trunks arrive.'

'Leaving so soon? Why, you just got here!'

'I cannot be long away from my estate. We shall make a more extended visit another time.'

'I hope so indeed. We don't see enough of Lizzie and her aunt. About the necklace – if you could find the original stones, I am still interested to buy it, Lizzie. The present time is not the best for me. I find myself a trifle short. If you are in dire need of funds. . . .' His eyes went quizzically to Sir Edmund.

'The situation is not desperate,' I assured him blithely, though it was certainly acute. I had not been allotting a proper amount of worry on that score.

We chatted on for a while. 'You will stay for luncheon at least,' Weston insisted. As there was no sign of Blount's carriage, we agreed to this.

'What would you like to do this morning?' Uncle asked politely.

It was settled that I would stroll through the park, Maisie

would write Jeremy a letter about our adventures, but
Edmund said nothing of his plans. I thought he might
accompany me, but he went to the study with Uncle
instead. He was amazingly stiff with me today. No more
show of being the loving fiancé. I could not imagine what
was bothering him. Even Maisie noticed it.

'What ails Sir Edmund?' she asked bluntly.

'I have no idea, unless he is unhappy to have to take us
to London.'

'You did nothing last night to offend him?'

'Certainly not. I am going to fetch Mitzi from the kitchen
to walk her. We don't want her too frisky in the carriage.'

In midmorning, the carriage and trunks arrived, allowing
us to make fresh toilettes. I was happy to get into clean
clothing and make a more decent appearance. I put on my
blue morning gown, then returned to the garden to await
luncheon. Mrs. Weston's one contribution to Rusholme
was a sort of replica of Ophelia's garden, to add her mite
to the Elizabethan theme. She had planted rosemary,
pansies, daisies, all bordered by the original roses. As I
strolled about trying to identify other flowers, Edmund
came to join me.

'Where's the dog?' was his welcoming speech. I had
turned Mitzi loose when I went to change. His using the
generic term for her indicated he was still in the boughs.

'Chasing rabbits, I believe.'

'It is a pity for us to be cooling our heels here. If we had
left early, we might have got to London by nightfall.'

His traveling mood had left him. There were definite
traces of a sulk around his lips. Nothing is less pleasant

than being cooped up in a carriage with a surly companion. I decided to cajole him back into humor.

'Cheer up, Sir Edmund. You might have excellent luck
at whatever inn we stop at tonight.'

'Meaning?' he asked, with a haughty stare.

'You know what I mean.'

The haughty stare was pushed perilously close to anger.
'I am not an *inveterate* libertine, you know.'

Of course not! It is only beyond the precincts of
Woldwood you behave like one. Come now, leave off sulking. Maisie has rung a peal over me for putting you out of
humor. If I am to be held t fault, you might at least tell me
what I have done.'

He made no immediate reply, but I noticed his eyes
were resting on the stupid little tin ring I wore. 'I am sorry
if I have inflicted my rude temper on you. I shall try to
behave better in future. Pretty garden,' he said, as a peace
offering, but remnants of pique remained.

'Is it that you want to get home? You did not plan on
such an extended leave when you set out for poor Willie's
wedding.'

That chance phrase, for some reason, brought a smile
back to his face.

'*Poor* Willie! I *do* pity him after all. You women are the
very devil,' he said, then laughed reluctantly.

'You didn't answer my question. *Are* you eager to get
home?'

'No, I am eager to meet Glandower Cummings, He is a
wretched fellow, you know. I have been chatting to your
uncle about him. The man holds him in high esteem, but

it seems to me he is nothing but an expensive worry. On top of it all, your uncle wants to adopt him legally. Your brother may kiss this estate goodbye.'

'He already has. It is his own he will be kissing goodbye if I don't find the diamonds.'

'How bad is the situation? Is Westgate actually in jeopardy?'

'I would not be selling my jewelry if it were not.'

'How does it come *you* are bailing Jeremy out? The necklace, I assume, is your dowry?'

'There is no need for a dowry when one does not intend to marry. Maisie and I live at Westgate; it is only fair I contribute to its upkeep. But my plan is to pay the mortgage installment; not the whole thing. I shall put the remainder in the funds.'

'If the place cannot carry itself, you are throwing good money after bad.'

'It could, if it were properly managed. We cannot let it go under. Where would we live, Maisie and I?'

'I take it the door to Eastgate is not irrevocably closed to you?'

'Is it possible you are suggesting I should marry Beattie?'

'Could, not should.'

'Oh, really, Edmund! He is old as the hills – older.'

'That is exactly the match to suit you, if you dislike marriage as much as you intimate. A gent who will pester you for a minimum length of time. He cannot have more than a few years left in him.'

'There are other impediments to the match,' I said, making light of it. 'Maisie is fond of him, you see. I would not want such stiff competition under my own roof.'

'Do you think she is fond of *me*?' he asked, with a strange little smile.

'Very much so. You stand second only to Beattie.'

'I shall try if I cannot dampen her ardor. Do you suppose the luncheon meat is burned yet? I am hungry enough to eat even the cinders your uncle considers edible.' Taking hold of my elbow, he led me indoors, with his humor restored.

The loving fiancé was highly evident over luncheon. Edmund ate up the cinders without a complaint. Many a solicitous inquiry for my preference between a pineapple and berries was heard, and soon a caring question as to when I would be ready to leave.

'Right away. We must eat and run, Uncle. I hope you can forgive our shabby manners.'

'Sir Edmund has promised to stop by on your wedding trip, Lizzie, so we shall have a better visit then.' Blount smiled blandly when I turned my astonished gaze on him.

'One-thirty already,' he said, drawing out his watch. 'We can make London tonight if we go hard at it. I'll keep fresh teams before us. We may have to drive past dark, but it will be worth it to have the trip done.'

The trunks were repacked, the carriage brought out, and we were off in a fine clatter of hooves, wheels and whip.

'We'll have an early crack at Glandower in the morning, Lizzie,' Edmund said. 'The more time we lose, the greater is the chance he will have unloaded your diamonds.'

'How should we approach him? We cannot barge in and accuse him of theft, with no evidence,' I pointed out.

'We require another plan, or another version of the same plan. Tell him Weston bought the necklace from you. If he still has it, he will be in a hurry to have a closer look at it. Maybe you could tell him you were carrying a copy in your reticule. That will make him look sharp.'

'This man is a genius,' Maisie informed me, vastly impressed with his ingenuity.

'Thank you, Maisie,' he smiled, then looked to see if I shared her enthusiasm.

'Maisie is becoming remarkably fond of you,' I cautioned.

'I better watch my step, eh?'

My aunt was as curious as anyone would be to hear meaningful remarks flung about her head, when the meaning was not clear to her. 'Edmund has taken the notion you are planning to wed him,' I said, to give some explanation. She is not the stiff sort who would object to bantering. She took it in good part.

'I might not say no if you offered, Sir Edmund,' she answered.

'Here, give her the tin ring,' I suggested, drawing it off, to reveal a green circle about my finger, but more importantly, an uncomfortable redness where its sharp edges were leaving their mark behind. 'Next time you become engaged not to be married, don't be so cheap, Edmund. Pay more than a crown for the tie that binds.'

'We'll get something better in London,' he answered matter of factly, sliding the ring into his pocket.

Maisie's eyes, bright with interest, flew to mine. His way of speaking was so *settled*-sounding that I too misunderstood him, and made a flaming jackass of myself. 'The charade is over now. I no longer require the ring. We are not really engaged,' I told him.

He blinked in amusement, looking from one to the other of us, reading on our faces as clearly as if we had spoken what we both thought, that the engagement had mysteriously become not a farce, but genuine. 'Surely you will not tell Glandower a different story than you told his stepfather? Till after we have met him, I must continue as your fiancé. Only for another day, Lizzie. Don't panic.'

If my face was not bright red, I would be much surprised. 'You don't have to go to the expense of buying a real ring for that,' I answered, trying to appear unconcerned.

'Buying? I had no idea of wasting my blunt. There are a couple of old rings floating around the London house somewhere. I seem to remember both my mother's and grandmother's are there. Of course, I shall want it back, as they have sentimental value to me.'

'Of course,' I answered airily.

He regarded me, the knowledge in his eyes confirming my fears. To set the cap on it, he shook his head in a disgusted way, as though to say – I am not caught, my girl. Don't think it.

I was obliged to make some fuss over my dog to divert attention from the awkward contretemps. 'I don't believe you bribed her with a beefsteak today, Edmund. She is not sitting on your knee, as I feared she would be,' I said, lifting her from her comfortable spot between our feet. She was not happy to be disturbed from her nap. She growled angrily.

'Let sleeping dogs lie,' Edmund suggested. It was good advice on more than one score.

It was not a particularly pleasant trip. Any innocent comment I made sounded as though I were harking back to the damnable subject of engagements. 'You hear that, Mitzi?' I asked my pug. 'He is through with you, fickle creature.' The instant it was out, I realized the double edge on the words. The look Edmund gave me fairly fulminated. After a few such unhappy starts, I sunk into silence. My companions too, while not actually dour, were not talkative. An occasional comment on some item of interest passed on the road was our only conversation.

It began to seem, after a few hours, as though we were all consigned to a traveling eternity in the oppressive quiet of the carriage. We stopped every few hours to change horses, usually taking advantage of it to stretch our legs, and once to refreshen ourselves with wine. At six-thirty, we were still several miles from London.

'We must be nearly there,' Maisie said hopefully, while her head wilted on her chest.

'Twelve or so miles yet,' Edmund replied. 'We'll take some dinner here for a break. My servants don't expect me, and will not be ready for company.'

Dinner was about the only pleasant interlude in the whole trip. We had a private parlor, small but very elegant. 'You will want to order a raw cow, Edmund, after being forced to eat cooked meat at Rusholme,' I mentioned.

'The hind quarter will do me. What would you ladies like – other than a comfortable bed I mean. For that we must wait a few more hours.'

We made our selections, and drank wine while awaiting delivery. We got through the entire meal without a single embarrassing word arising. We discussed current events, plays, books, music, like any civilized group out for an evening's pleasure. Edmund got the latest newspapers from London to see what entertainment offered in the city, after we had completed the business that was our main object. I could not feel we would be in a mood for much enjoyment if the outcome were not successful, but our host refused to consider that possibility.

'We'll get him, never fear. If he has already hawked it, we'll get it back from the culprit he sold it to. It has to be there. He knew you were traveling with it, he had left Rusholme in time to intercept you en route, and he has a wall-eyed valet.'

'I wonder why he had the copy made,' Maisie said. 'He knew from Weston's copy what it looked like. Why make a copy, only to take to a pawn shop as soon as he stole the original?'

'He didn't have a copy made. Weston had two. Did I not mention it?' Edmund asked. 'It came up during our chat in his study. I told him we had seen a copy in Reuben's window – just casually mentioned it as a curious incident, and he explained how he thinks it came there. Six months ago, he took the idea to have all his Elizabethan jewels duplicated, as he is frequently asked to loan them to museums and things and dislikes to send out the genuine articles. He packed them up in a chest and took them to Hamlet in London. The copy of your necklace was in with the rest. Hamlet apparently thought he was to make a copy of the copy as well, and did it. Of course Weston had no need for two copies, and gave the second to his housekeeper for a trinket. The housekeeper is Greenie's aunt. I found an opportunity to speak to her about it before we left. She gave it to Greenie. He hinted for it, pretending he wished to give it to some girl he was chasing. He went to see her, according to the story, while Glandower was visiting at Rusholme. But instead of giving it to his girl, he obviously hawked it at Winchester.'

'Why did you not tell us sooner?' I demanded.

'Your uncle didn't want me to. He was upset when I told him about the copy in the pawn shop. He did not say so, but I think he believes Glandower is up to something. He harked back to Lizzie changing the stones in her necklace, wondered that I had allowed – that is, that I had not subsidized you, if you were put to such shifts to make ends meet. In short, he smells a rat in our story, but cannot quite locate it. His major concern is that you not have a poor opinion of Glandower – especially *you*, Liz. I hesitated to open my budget to you, but as you already know him for a thief, it is hardly a breach of confidence to confirm it.'

'You might as well tell us the whole. Did you tell him we think Glandower had the thing stolen?' I asked frankly.

'No, but it wouldn't surprise me much if he knows it. He was wretchedly embarrassed. He feels fatherly toward the boy. That is when he told me he means to adopt him.'

'Why would he want to do that?' Maisie asked, her moon face screwed up in consternation.

'Everyone needs someone to love and feel responsible for,' Edmund suggested. 'When a human being cannot be found to fill the role, some ladies sink to taking on a dog, or a cat,' he added, with a pointed look in my own direction.

'Or a herd of cows,' I retaliated.

'*I* never felt it necessary,' Maisie told us.

'Did you not, Aunt? Jeremy would be amazed to hear you say so. If you have not legally adopted him, you have done everything else but.'

'He loves the boy. That is the only explanation,' Edmund said simply. 'When love flies in the window, common sense flies out the door, to rephrase an old saw. I refer, of course, to paternal love in this case.'

'A pity some filial love had not been returned. I would dearly love to whip Glandower Cummings till he wipes that grin off his face,' Maisie said angrily.

'He won't be grinning when we get through with him,' Edmund promised. 'Shall we take Mitzi for her walk before resuming our journey, Liz?'

'No, let us get on with this interminable trip.'

'She's getting pretty frisky,' he cautioned, but as I looked toward the corner, I saw her to be settled in comfortably with a bone, which I had not seen Edmund slip to her, so slyly had he done it.

I took the idea he wanted to speak to me privately, possibly about something else Weston had said. 'Very well, but let us make it a short walk.'

'We'll be right back, Maisie,' he said. 'I'll settle our account here on the way out. Join me in two minutes, Liz.'

My aunt and I discussed this new revelation as I put on my jacket and bonnet, and I leashed Mitzi. My aunt had nothing but abuse for Glandower, but to tell the truth, I was beginning to feel sorry for the boy. He was all but caught, and in addition to the disgrace and criminal reprisals, he would lose the love and respect of his stepfather. I pitied Weston too. What could have caused the boy to go so wrong? Uncle was generous to a fault with him, gave him enormous sums to pay his debts. He had either fallen into some monumental hobble, or he was just plain evil. I did not remember him as being actually *evil*.

If I had taken Blount's advice and used two minutes to put on my bonnet, instead of one, he would have been spared his shame. When I went into the lobby, he was chatting with a lady of questionable virtue – again. It is shocking the way they are taking over the public inns. I stood a few yards from them, watching but unable to hear their words. I saw him shake his head and make some smiling demurral. As he did so, he cast a cautious eye toward our parlor, and saw me looking at him. I know he wanted to kill me. Such a black look as I was subjected to. I had made enough of a fool of myself for one day. Not a word would I say about it. I prolonged the drawing on of my gloves till she had walked away. Only then did I advance to him.

'All set?' I asked, taking the arm he offered.

We went out into the street. 'Which way shall we go?' he asked, looking up and down.

'Mitzi has decided we go left,' I answered, as she took a flying start in that direction, pulling me after her.

'Shall I hold the leash for you?' he offered.

'No, I can manage her.'

The darkness had descended to the point where the shop windows were no attraction. The wares had become invisible. We walked half a block in silence, then Edmund said, 'That wasn't what you think,' in a defensive way.

'You don't know what I think. *I* thought the vicar's wife you were speaking to was asking direction, to the closest cathedral.'

'She accosted me. I didn't go after her.'

'Of course not. How should you go after a perfectly respectable woman?' And why should you feel accountable to *me* if you had, my tone implied.

He decided to abandon this topic. 'Not afraid to drive after dark, are you?' was his next venture.

'No, I have never been held up by highwaymen. Was that what you meant?'

'Yes. I am not at all sure it was wise to take two ladies on a journey at night. It would not delay us much to stay over and leave early in the morning.'

'I thought you wanted to get to London tonight.'

'We would make better time in daylight.'

'No, no, let us continue on. I have already been robbed of my valuables, and you can stick your roll of money into your boot.'

'First place they look.'

'In your hat then.'

'The second place they look.'

'As you are familiar with the places they look, hide it where they do not.'

We took only a short walk before going quickly back to the inn. The female was still loitering about the lobby. She looked to Edmund with a questioning smile. I understood at once his eagerness to be attacked by highwaymen.

'We shall stay overnight if you wish, Sir Edmund,' I said, with a level glance at the woman. 'I misunderstood your desire to remain.'

He pulled his lips into a thin line and pounced so swiftly to our parlor he nearly pulled my arm from its socket. 'We're ready, Maisie,' he said in a remarkably angry voice. She already had on her hat.

'What is he in a pucker about now?' she asked, when he went out to order our carriage.

'He is miffed that I insisted on continuing the trip tonight.'

'Why, *he* was the one who wanted to go on.'

'Something must have come up to change his mind.'

'What have you been up to *now*, Lizzie?'

'Don't ask, or I might be tempted to tell you.'

The first part of the voyage was a conversationalist's delight compared to the last. My aunt took to snoring softly, while Sir Edmund folded his arms over his chest, leaned back in a corner and sulked. I lifted my pug to my knee and stroked her to sleep, as quiet as the others. There was only one disturbance. In about half an hour, we heard some shouting ahead of us on the road.

'Highwaymen!' Edmund shouted jubilantly, while a wave of fear whipped through me.

'Have you hidden your money?' I asked him.

'In my boot.'

'That's the first place they'll look!'

'I haven't enough to worry about. It has been an expensive trip,' he added curtly.

So it had too. He had not planned to jaunter about the countryside for days with two women and a dog, hiring teams and paying for the repair of two carriages. 'Be sure to give me the reckoning when we get home. I do not bank in London.'

The shouts, as we learned when we reached their source, were occasioned by a pair of drunkards straggling down the road, singing and abusing each other at the top of their lungs. 'Your hope of highwaymen has been disappointed,' I told him smugly.

'I am inured to having my hopes disappointed,' he replied in his put-upon tone.

It was the last speech any of us made before we rattled up in front of his house in Belgrave Square much later. It was a fine home, but it elicited no praise from me. 'Is this it?' I asked with an air of indifference.

'No, this is Carlton House,' was his sarcastic answer. His mood had not improved over the length of the trip. The house was in total darkness. Had he not had a key with him, we would have been sunk, but he had. He let us in, Maisie and I walking softly, so as not to disturb the sleeping servants. He felt around on a hall table for a tinder box, lit some candles, took one up, and strode off into the black bowels of the place. When he returned, he said, 'My housekeeper will be here shortly to show you to your rooms. If you need anything, do not hesitate to tell her.'

'You shouldn't have bothered rousing her up, Edmund,' Maisie said, stifling a yawn.

'She is paid to look after me,' was his unfeeling answer.

The woman, when she came, was neither surprised nor offended to be hauled from her bed at so late an hour. She took us abovestairs to our chambers. Edmund came up at our heels.

'Do you mind if Mitzi sleeps in my room, or would you prefer to put her somewhere else?' I asked him.

'Suit yourself, but pray do not let her destroy the room.'

'What time shall we leave in the morning?' I asked, not rising to his insults. As though I would let my pug destroy another's property!

'I have decided to go alone to Glandower's place. I got you into this mess, and I shall rectify it.'

'It is not your fault – not entirely. If he was intent on robbing me, he would have found a means, even without the accident.'

'I accept full responsibility. If I cannot retrieve the necklace, I shall reimburse you for it. I begin to wish I had thought of that simple expedient at the outset.' The whole conversation was more of an angry harangue than anything else. 'Five thousand, was it?'

'Thirty-five hundred, and you are not paying for it.'

His jaws stiffened, but he said nothing. He looked like nothing so much as a sulking boy. I knew why he was in this pelter, too. 'If you felt so strongly about remaining overnight at the inn, you should have said so,' I finally told him. I had been longing to say it for hours. 'The delay would have been preferable to this show of boorishness.'

He drew a long, slow breath, while his temper came to a rolling boil. 'You are *determined* to confirm your first poor opinion of me. I *told* you. . . .'

'Never mind. It is nothing to me.'

'You have made that more than obvious. Goodnight, ma'am. I shall in all probability be gone when you arise in the morning. I hope to have your necklace back to you by noon.'

'I am going with you!'

'No, Miss Braden, you are not,' he contradicted, then strode down the hall with his fists clenched at his sides.

CHAPTER 12

We left for Glandower Cummings's place, Edmund and myself, at nine-thirty. By morning, his ranting fury had dissipated to simple anger, a comparatively good mood for him. I was in no hurry to go downstairs, for I did not awaken till nearly nine, and was sure he would be gone. Truth to tell, I was not overly eager to confront Cummings. I had decided, during a fairly sleepless night, to let Blount go alone and handle it if he could. He sat at the breakfast table, quite obviously waiting for me, as his plate was empty of beefsteak. A newspaper was propped before him, indicating a leisurely meal.

'Good morning,' I said, adopting a cheerful tone, and refraining from any mention of his not being off after Glandower.

'Good morning,' he answered, lowering the newspaper. His face wore a sheepish expression. I took the idea he was ashamed of his evening's performance, as well he might be. 'Let me pour you some coffee while you wait for breakfast.'

He rang a bell, which brought a servant scrambling to our side.

'Where is Mitzi?' he asked.

'Your butler was kind enough to tend to her for me. You will be relieved to hear she has not demolished your chamber.'

'I am afraid I was not in the best of moods last night.'

'If that is your second best, Edmund, you ought to buy a desert island and set up as a hermit.'

'I had a touch of migraine,' he said, clutching at that limp old excuse for ill manners.

'Pity. You are subject to frequent attacks, I think? You really ought to have your head looked at.'

'By a mental doctor, you mean?'

'Of course.'

My civility won a reluctant smile. 'The attacks are frequent, but of short duration. A good night's sleep will usually cure them. Do you still want to come with me to confront Cummings? It will not be pleasant. But then I have observed you are not one to shrink from unpleasant encounters.'

'Very true, I encounter a deal of unpleasantness in my dealings with gentlemen.'

'Do you suppose there could be something amiss in your handling of gentlemen, that you encounter so much unpleasantness?' he suggested, but in a bantering way, determined not to come to cuffs again.

'Yes, I believe I am much too polite with them.'

'Much,' he agreed at once. 'I have been struck from the beginning by your excessive politeness. To *me*, in any case. Did you beat me over the head with your reticule when I overturned your carriage? Certainly not. You couldn't find it. You ordered me into the ditch to look for it instead, then were so polite as to accuse me of common thievery, to order me to empty my pockets for inspection, as though you were a Bow Street Runner and I a criminal.'

'*You* accused the squire,' I reminded him.

'At whose instigation?'

'Besides, I got you out of jail, didn't I?'

'Certainly you did, Lady Elizabeth, by bandying my name about in a most unnecessary way. You were very kind, too, in insisting I go *twice* into the wilds to visit Reuben. I want you to know I appreciate how deeply I am in your debt.'

'Should I awaken Maisie?' I asked, to stem the flow of memories.

'Suit yourself. You always do.' A pugnacious tone was creeping into his words. I ignored it, also the sleeping Maisie.

'Your migraine is returning, is it?' was all I said.

'No. Lizzie, I am determined not to have a headache today. Here,' he said, tossing a gold ring down on the table. 'We are engaged again. Sufficient cause for a bout of the megrim. Don't lose it. It is my mother's.'

'I won't. And I won't let Mitzi eat it either. It is too small,' I said, trying to push it over my knuckle.

'My mother was small.'

'Was she?' I asked, surprised. I had envisioned her a large, loud-voiced grenadier of a woman. When a man is opposed to marriage, it will sometimes be due to a quarrelsome mama, I have discovered. Then, too, his own characteristics had to be inherited from either her or his father. 'What was she like?'

'A saint. Patient, forebearing. She had plenty to bear. My father was like me. You look surprised. Have I said something to indicate she was ill-natured?'

'No, not at all.'

'She had a hard life. A foul-tempered husband is a sad infliction to spring on an unsuspecting lady.'

'Was she unsuspecting? An arranged marriage, I deduce?'

'No, they had been neighbors forever, but I shouldn't think he showed her his worst side when they were courting. She always looked – frightened, or abused. Unhappy is all I mean. He didn't actually harm her physically. She was gentle, easily provoked to tears. She cried a good deal.'

She sounded a perfect ninnyhammer to me, or worse, a female who used her tears to bring her spouse round her thumb. 'I expect that brought a halt to your father's tantrums?' I asked.

'Instantly! My father knew two moods – anger and remorse. I think it is a mistake for a man of unstable temperament to marry, don't you?'

'To marry a timid lady, yes. Good gracious, is *this* the reason you espouse misogamy? Don't be such a gudgeon, Edmund. Find someone who is not afraid of your blustering, arm her with a stout club and marry her.'

'Omitting the stout club, I feel you may be right.'

'Omitting the club, I am not at all sure I am right. I

cannot get her ring on,' I said, after pushing at it for some moments.

'Rub a little of this butter on your finger,' he suggested.

The trick worked. It slid on, without quite cutting off my circulation. 'Let us decide exactly how to proceed with Glandower,' I said. 'Do we pretend it is a social call merely, and tell him Weston bought my necklace?'

'I have been revising our strategy. As we will not be putting up with Cummings, a search of his premises will not be at all easy to arrange. Then too, if he has already pawned the necklace, we are at point *non plus*. Even if he shows surprise at his stepfather's purchase, he will not likely crop out into a confession. We may be morally certain he is guilty, but to prove it is more difficult.'

'Unless we could learn where he sold it.'

'Precisely. What we should do is tour the jewel merchants as a couple of connoisseurs looking for old jewelry. Your piece is interesting enough that word of its presence might well be known in the traders' circle. At least I always know within a day when a neighbor has bought a new bull – I daresay it is no different with diamonds. If we can discover who bought it, then it will not be impossible to get a description of the seller.'

'We know his description: a wall-eyed man in a green jacket.'

Edmund shook his head. 'No. Bibelots of no great value will be purchased from a commoner. Glandower would more likely have traded off the real diamonds himself. A trader would not buy them from just anyone, unless he is an outright crook.'

'This plan will take a while to accomplish. It presup-
poses as well that Glandower *has* sold them. How many
traders do you reckon there are in London?'

'Dozens, probably hundreds. My hope is that we will not
have to visit them all. If the piece is in town, I expect any
of the large traders can direct us to its purchaser.'

'It won't do any harm to try. If we hear nothing, then we
will assume Cummings has not sold it yet, and confront
him.'

When Maisie joined us later, she approved of the plan.
She also agreed to remain at his home while we two spent
the morning tracking down dealers in secondhand gems.
Hamlet, who is jokingly called the Prince of Denmark by
his clients, had his shop at the corner of Cranbourne Alley.
It was stuffed full of gold and silver plate in one room,
while the jewel room held a king's ransom in all manner of
precious stone, but it held no necklace given to Sir Eldridge
by Queen Elizabeth, nor had he any rumors of the object
being in town. He gave a list of likely dealers, with Rundell
and Bridges at the top of the list. The shop held less
opulent objects than Hamlet's, but it displayed them more
attractively. My necklace was not there either, but the
dealer had heard some talk of it, which sounded promising. To save needless time, Edmund, who was familiar with
the city, laid out a map for us that would involve a minimum of doubling back and forth. We settled on a story we
would relate to the dealers, one that limited our interest to
that one specific necklace and also included our eagerness
to get it immediately. Our imaginary engagement was
rushed into an imaginary wedding. Pampered bride that I

was, I would have nothing but an Elizabethan diamond necklace for my wedding present, during our brief honeymoon in London. My doting spouse tried to act besotted enough to make this tale credible. His temper made his job difficult, but my assertive way was of great help in my role.

'This will save us hours of looking at other pieces,' Edmund pointed out. 'They will be trying to unload rings and brooches and bracelets on me if I indicate an interest in old jewelry in general. It is only a necklace you want, Lady Blount.'

'What an ugly-sounding name it is.'

He looked shocked. 'Even my mother, who objected to everything else she married into, never objected to her name,' he answered.

'Perhaps her maiden name was equally ugly. Mine is not.'

'You won't have to change your initial at least,' he answered reasonably.

'I hadn't planned to reembroider my handkerchiefs for one morning's use,' I told him.

We spent a grueling morning trekking from shop to shop. They were too close together to bother with the carriage, and really too far apart to walk. Inquiring for one specific necklace did not save us from having to examine every other sort of jewel either. Anything in the shop that was more than ten years old was brought out for my delectation. Our travels were leading us to the east of the city.

'Glandower lives on Downing Street,' I reminded Blount. 'Let us return to that general vicinity at least.'

'He would be more likely to have peddled it farther from

home,' he reminded.

'No one has seen it. I begin to think he didn't sell it at all, but kept it to wear himself.'

'He must have needed the blunt desperately to have stolen it. If he needed the money, then he hawked the necklace. It is only a matter of time.'

'Time and place. Humor me, Edmund. Don't be so cruel to your blushing bride. Hire a cab and let us go back to civilization, try some of the shops close to Downing Street.'

'Are you tired?'

'No, exhausted. These heeled slippers were not made for hiking, but sitting in a carriage.'

'I'll take you home and come back out this afternoon myself.'

'I require only a respite, not retirement.'

After repeated hectorings, I convinced him to hire a cab. 'Let us dismount near Glandower's house, and try the places closest to it,' I suggested.

The list of names and addresses was examined. The closest was not so very close. Instead of going to Downing Street, we were let off on the south end of Bond. The first shop we entered had been offered the necklace, but had not met the gentleman's price. A request for a description of 'the gentleman' gave us a fair picture of Glandower. Tall, rather thin, young, with fair hair. A good-looking chap. 'One would not have taken him for Polish,' the shopkeeper finished up casually.

'Polish?' I asked, staring at this new twist.

'The Polish ambassador's cousin was the man I refer to. The diamonds came into his family on the maternal side, grandmother, an Englishwoman. Baron Czarnkow is very sorry to have to part with it, but he is in the suds. Gambling.'

'You wouldn't know who he took it to after he left here?' Edmund asked, ignoring Glandower's new nationality and title.

'I directed him to Newington. He handles more antiques than I do myself. There is not a great demand for antique jewelry. We do a better job on the stones nowadays. I have a very pretty. . . .'

'Thank you. My wife is determined on that particular necklace,' Edmund said, scanning his list for Newington's address.

Newington had not met Baron Czarnkow's price either, but the man to whom he sent us was even then negotiating the deal. Not to say Mr Anthony had the necklace in his shop, but he had made an offer which the Baron was graciously considering. Czarnkow had expressed some intention of returning soon.

'So he hasn't sold it yet,' Edmund said, happy to have at least this atom of success to the morning's strenuous endeavors.

'Or hasn't bothered to tell Mr Anthony in any case,' I pointed out.

Edmund turned around and darted back inside. When he came out, he was smiling. 'Yesterday afternoon the Baron was still negotiating,' he announced triumphantly.

'Good, then he has had only this morning to unload it. I hope he sleeps in late.'

'Gamblers usually do.'

'Shall we go directly to Downing Street then? Edmund – I think we ought to go to a magistrate and get a search warrant. Take a Runner with us, not give him a chance to hide it on us.'

He stopped walking. There in the middle of the street he began rubbing his chin and frowning. 'That would make it so very public. Bring a scandal and disgrace down on his head. Not that I give a tinker's curse about that grinner of a Glandower, but your uncle deserves better.'

I sighed wearily, trying to decide on the best course, but one that left no chance of losing out on the necklace at this late point in our chase.

'You are worn to a thread, Lizzie,' he said, examining my face. 'I am taking you home.'

'What are *you* going to do?'

'Go to my bank. Traveling with you is very dear.'

'You are not going to *buy* the necklace!'

'Oh, no, I am going to win it. He loses to everyone else at cards. Why not me? All I require is a stake, to set up a game.'

'You don't know him. How can you set up a game with a total stranger?'

'Use your wits, Lady Blount. That is the last time you will hear the ugly name today. We are now not only unmarried, unengaged, but total strangers. Brace yourself for one final challenge. You and Maisie must go to him and tell him of the theft. Also let him know you have been touring the shops, to ensure his not selling the thing this afternoon. Discover his plans for the day and night, and I shall arrange to bump into him somewhere, and try for a game tonight.'

'Maisie was right. You *are* cagey.'

'Genius was the word used. I believe she exaggerated a little.'

'It is myself who ought to be a genius. How can I find out, on a mere social visit, what his plans are for the day? I can hardly subject him to a direct quiz without his becoming suspicious.'

'You could roll your big, bright eyes at him, Liz. Let him squire you somewhere or other, tell me the destination, and I shall undertake to be there. I'll scrape an acquaintance somehow, never fear.'

'Failing all else, you can always run him off the road. That results in delightful friendships, does it not?'

'Delightful. We'll hail a cab and go to pick up Maisie. If you cannot charm Cummings into an outing with you, be sure to discover what he plans to do instead. The two important points are to make sure he knows he cannot hawk the necklace, and to discover his plans. Under no circumstance are you to give my name or description, as I do not want him to know I have anything to do with you.'

I had removed my gloves and was trying to pull off his mother's ring. 'I cannot get it off,' I said.

'Do you think the Fates are trying to tell you something?'

'Yes, that I was a fool to ever put it on in the first place. All this pulling is swelling my knuckle too. It is beginning to hurt.'

'Stop fiddling with it. Glandower won't notice it.'

A cab pulled up to us. We got in and went to Belgrave Square. Within minutes, Maisie and myself were being rushed out the door into Blount's own black carriage, which was considered safely anonymous enough to drive to Downing Street.

'Come straight home after. I'll be waiting on thorns for my instructions,' Sir Edmund said, drawing out his watch to time us.

'Put away your watch, Edmund. You will have an hour or more off the treadwheel. Relax.'

He looked confused. Relaxing was as alien to him as flying.

CHAPTER 13

My aunt and I were shown into Glandower Cummings's apartment by a general factotum wearing a green jacket and a pair of wall-eyes. It took a strong exertion of will power not to accuse the man on the spot. We were left to cool our heels in a very mediocre parlor while Glandower was called. I am pretty sure we had him roused out of his bed. When he came to us, not quite grinning but trying to look happy to see us, he had taken time to perform his toilette. He looked and smelled like a seven-day beau. The stench of Steak's lavender water was overpowering. So was his jacket. It was of blue Bath cloth, sporting four of the largest brass buttons ever seen outside of a circus. His blond curls sat in wanton disarray on his white forehead. His blue eyes were half closed. There was a certain wariness in his manner – the only indication he was guilty of anything.

'Good morning, Glandower,' I said cheerfully. 'You will be surprised to see us, when Uncle Weston told you we were to visit *him*.'

'What happened?' he asked, trying to contain his interest within decorous bounds, but already sounding worried.

I told him my tale of stolen gems, saying nothing of either Sir Edmund or wall-eyed suspects. 'We have concluded someone stole them and is trying to sell them here in London, so we spent our morning touring all the jewelry shops,' I said. 'If the wretch *did* sell them, I shall get his description, and call in Bow Street.'

He expressed as much interest as he dared in the business. We discussed it for a while, then discussed other family matters, while I mentally framed questions that would discover his afternoon's plans.

'We have had a very tedious morning. I think we have earned a little entertainment this afternoon. What do you suggest, Glandower?'

'I am not fit for much,' Maisie said.

'There is not much an unaccompanied lady can do by herself,' Glandower pointed out. 'Will you accept my escort, Lizzie? I will be happy to show you around the town.'

'I'm sure you have more interesting things to do than squire me,' I told him, attempting a coquettish smile.

'Not at all. I would be happy to be your escort.'

'All right then, but I think I should go to Bow Street first, and report my stolen goods,' I said, to watch him squirm.

'Let me do it for you,' he volunteered with suspicious alacrity. 'It is unpleasant work for a lady. I have all the details, and know precisely what the necklace looks like, so there is no problem in it.'

'Oh, would you?' I asked, batting my lashes furiously. Indeed he would! He was all manly protection and concern. As soon as he had done so, he would call for me and take me for a drive. The next question sent me stuttering.

'What hotel are you staying at?' he asked.

'Hotel?' I asked blankly.

Maisie saved the day. 'The Clarendon,' she answered quickly.

'Excellent. I shall pick you up there in, say, an hour?'

'Make it an hour and a half,' I said. 'Where shall we go?' Edmund, of course, had to know this.

'Where would you like to go? It is a fine day for a drive.'

The streets of the city offered little scope for Edmund to meet my escort. 'Richmond Hill?' I suggested hesitantly.

'That is fine with me. I haven't been there in an age.'

We had a glass of wine, and then our carriage was called. 'I blush to tell Edmund he must hire us yet another room at a hotel,' I said, as we hastened back to Belgrave Square. 'I have lost track of how much I owe him.'

'I don't believe he's counting,' she responded, with a sly smile.

'*You* are an excellent cipherer, Aunt. You keep tabs for me.'

'Do I include the various rings he has given you?' she asked.

'Oh, no, they were his own idea. Besides, they are only on loan.'

'You know, Liz, even if we get the necklace back, we will

still be in the basket, with Weston not anxious to buy it at this time.'

'I wonder if Edmund would be interested to purchase it,' I said. It was only a passing thought, spoken aloud, but it brought her wrath down on my head.

Edmund had luncheon awaiting when we returned home. 'How did it go? Did you hook him?' he asked eagerly.

'It was like stealing candy from a baby.'

'Or diamonds from Miss Braden,' he threw in, quite unnecessarily. 'Where is the rendezvous to be?'

'He is taking me to Richmond Hill,' I said, then sat wording my next speech more carefully. 'Of course, I could not ask him to pick me up here. I could not mention your name.'

'Where are you meeting him?' he asked.

'At the Clarendon Hotel. I told him we are putting up there. I hope it is not terribly expensive to hire a room for a day?'

His dispirited sigh told me I was out in my hope. 'The Pulteney is more expensive. How does it come you did not tell him the *most* expensive place in town?'

'I didn't know which one that was.'

I received one of his hawklike glares. 'I'll take you over to the Clarendon after lunch. Maisie accompanies you?'

'To the hotel, not on the drive. We are leaving very soon. We had better eat.'

There was little eaten by anyone save our host. His cook had been serving raw meat for too long. Even an order to have it well-done resulted in no more than a quick flash of our steak over a flame. I was too excited to enjoy food in any case. There was a delicious excitement in the charade that lay before us. I do not often leave Westgate, or want to, but I knew I would find its pleasures dull after this eventful interlude.

We made a hasty meal, with Edmund's watch propped beside his cup for constant timing; an even hastier dash to the Clarendon, to get installed in a chamber about twenty minutes before Glandower tapped at the door. 'Why must you always *hurry* so?' I asked him.

'We wouldn't want to be *late!*' was the only answer he had.

He was still in the room when Glandower's knock came at the door. He jumped into the clothes-press to hide. Fortunately it held no clothing.

'What time will you be back?' Maisie asked before we left. She would want to know how long she must sit in tedious quiet in the room, or perhaps she planned to return to Belgrave Square and wished to know at what time she must be back on the job.

'Before dark,' Glandower answered vaguely.

'Earlier than that, Aunt. By six,' I clarified, so she could make her plans accordingly.

Cummings had a dashing sporting curricle with a mischievous team of grays harnessed up to it. He made some effort to be entertaining as we drove at a smart clip to Richmond Hill. He referred voluntarily to the matter of the stolen necklace.

'I took time to dash to a few spots I know that buy used jewelry before I picked you up,' he told me. 'One of them thinks he might have a line on the goods. I plan to go back to him tomorrow morning. If he has the necklace, I'll call in Bow Street, and let you know, of course.'

'You haven't been to Bow Street yet then?' I asked. I was surprised, not that he had not been, but that he admitted it.

'I was halfway there, and then thought it might be faster to try my hand at a few shops I know. We can go to Bow Street now, if you like.'

I was beginning to have second thoughts about Glandower. It occurred to me he might have decided to turn honest, as the cards were not in his favor. Was it possible he meant to 'discover' my necklace at a shop, and get it returned to me? I realized then that this was my hope. It was wretched of him to have stolen it, but Weston was building his life around the scoundrel, and I could not like to hurt an old man. I spoke a few harsh words of the reprisals awaiting anyone who ventured on a life of crime.

'Such villains deserve the worst treatment. Whipping is too good for them,' he seconded me, with every appearance of sincerity.

This morose pall lightened as we approached Richmond Hill. One would have to be an ascetic not to adore the spot, so charming with its gardens, water, and pavilions. We stopped halfway up the hill to view the Terrace Gardens, very pretty in the summer sunlight, though Glandower thought the flowers would be more profuse in the spring. After an examination of the Gardens and the mansions around us, we proceeded to the top of the hill. Cummings was not impressed by the Star and Garter

Hotel, which alone was worth the trip in my estimation. It resembled some stately French chateau, and had a fancy Italian terraced garden too.

I had not realized Richmond Park was such a large affair, much too enormous to be likely to bump into Edmund, with no fixed meeting place designated. There were thousands upon thousands of acres of water, parks, gardens, buildings, even a forest.

'What do people usually go to see when they come here?' I asked, hoping to hear of some popular meeting spot, such as the barrier at Hyde Park.

'Some of them take a boat out, some of them tour the Gardens, usually everyone ends up here, at the Star and Garter, sooner or later.'

In the normal way, I would have expected Edmund *sooner*, but as he was obliged to leave after us, he would not be here before us. 'Let us roam around for a while, then come back later for a drink,' I suggested.

We strolled through the park to admire the rolling hills, the groves of oaks, the fern. The view from Broomfield Hill, also some of the other hills, was magnificent. Glandower told me that in the distance you could see as far as Surrey, Dorking Gap. It was not necessary for him to tell me it was also an extremely fatiguing pastime, climbing hills, for he had stabled his carriage at the hotel. After an hour of sightseeing, we had not begun to cover the area, but were ready for something to quench our thirst.

As we walked and roamed, I found myself making the quite dreadful mistake of getting to know Glandower better than I had before, and *liking* him. He was truly trying to entertain me; he was sensitive to beauty, informed of the history of the place we visited. He seemed strangely wistful, which I interpreted as remorse of his guilty conscience.

'It is beautiful. What a good time you must have, Glandower, living in London, with freedom and access to all these spots.'

'You tire of it after a while,' he said.

'I suppose one does. Why do you not find something useful to do then? Make a career for yourself, if you are becoming bored.'

'I would like to. I am seeking work at Whitehall, but it does not pay well, you know, and besides I don't expect I will be much good at it.'

'Surely Uncle gives you an allowance.'

'Yes, oh, yes! He is very generous, but. . . .'

But he gambled it away. My pity lessened. 'Your expenses as a bachelor cannot be great.'

'No, the thing is. . . .' He stopped, becoming shy.

'What is it?' I prodded gently.

'The thing is, cousin, I would like not to be a bachelor. There is a girl I would like to marry. Miss Millington, from back home, but how could I support her?'

'Why do you not take her to Rusholme?'

'Rusholme?' he asked, startled. 'I couldn't do that. Mr Braden is only my stepfather. Since mama's death, I don't spend much time there. Duty visits only, to keep in touch. No, it would be presumptuous of me to land a wife in on him.'

'He would *love* it!'

'No, really! I am not on such terms of intimacy with him

that I could do anything of the sort. I shall keep looking for something in the city. Something that pays more than a hundred guineas per annum,' he said, but with a resigned to failure sort of a slump to his shoulders.

What he really wished to discuss was not work or Rusholme, but Miss Millington. After assuring me she was not a great heiress or beauty, he went on to discuss such clouds of Titian hair, such large and lustrous hazel eyes, such a pretty little nose and unequaled smile that I was given to understand only a blind man would not find her an Incomparable. Her mind too, while not at all intellectual, seemed to have plumbed the depths of all philosophy. Only her dowry was unchanged – still inadequate.

'I would at least discuss going to Rusholme with Mr Braden,' I insisted. 'You would be no end of help to him, take over the reins of Rusholme gradually, as he is getting old. His gout bothers him a good deal lately. He would be grateful for your help.'

'What help could I give him? I know nothing of farming. Besides. . . .'

'What bothers you?'

'He would take the idea I was hinting for the place, thinking to inherit it. It will go to your brother, Lizzie. I am surprised you urge me to ingratiate myself.'

A quick spurt of selfish hope that Jeremy might yet inherit warred with my growing like for Glandower. I had to remind myself he was a thief and a gambler, for my instinct was to press him to go home. 'Nothing is settled in that respect,' was my comment.

He regarded me, his eyes alive with interest, but said

nothing. I figured enough time had passed that Edmund would be at the Star and Garter. If he was not there, I had absolutely no notion how to find him. I realized we ought to have made our meeting place more definite, and blamed it on him we had not, as I was not aware how huge the area was.

We tracked back to the hotel. As we approached the door, Mitzi came racing forward to meet me. I did not know Edmund meant to bring her along, but it was quite as ingenious as any of his other ideas. It made an excellent excuse for him to accost us. I made a great fuss over my pug, patting her, and fearing her friendliness would alert Glandower we were not strangers.

Blount strolled over to us, apologizing for the outrageous manners of his mutt. 'I was given her by a friend, who did an inferior job of training her,' he said, taking advantage of it to get in a dig at me.

'I disagree. She is charming and so friendly,' I retaliated.

We proceeded to some exchange of remarks upon Richmond Hill and its beauties. Edmund soon introduced himself as Mr Haskins, and a relative stranger to the city. He inquired of Glandower, who was by then established as an inhabitant, what he might suggest for an evening's entertainment.

Plays, musical shows, concerts and lectures were mentioned, all of which Sir Edmund listened to without any interest at all. 'Did you have something specific in mind?' Glandower asked.

'As a matter of fact, I had,' he admitted. 'I was hoping to get in on a card game. I do not belong to any of the clubs. Do you know of a private place that will accept a stranger, providing he is well inlaid?'

Cummings mentioned two such dens, but still Edmund frowned and was dissatisfied. 'A friendly game with just a couple of fellows was what I had in mind,' he suggested.

'Where are you putting up, Mr Haskins?' Cummings asked. 'If I hear of a private game, I'll send you word.'

'The Clarendon,' he answered, perhaps because he already had a room there.

'That is where *I* am staying,' I said, smiling like a regular hick.

'I think I can help you,' Glandower told him, his eyes running over Edmund to judge him for potential pickings. His tailoring was expensive, his general getup that of a gentleman of fashion. 'Yes, I'll leave an address off. Give the fellow at the door my name. He'll make you welcome, Mr Haskins.'

'Will you be part of the game yourself, sir?' Edmund inquired in a friendly, not overly curious manner.

'I thought you might like to go to a theater tonight, Lizzie?' Cummings said, making it a question.

I knew what was expected of me. 'No, Maisie and I plan an early night. She is a trifle upset with the accident still. I shall stay at the hotel and bear her company.'

'In that case, I expect you will see me this evening,' Glandower said to Edmund.

Edmund expressed his pleasure, made his adieux, then left. Mitzi remained behind, pawing at my skirt in the hope of being carried.

I was obliged to call after him. 'Mr Haskins! You have

forgotten your dog!'

Blount covered his gaffe with his usual ingenuity. 'Forgotten her? Why the truth of the matter is, I hoped I might manage to lose her. She is the worst infliction ever saddled on a man. I place the blame square on her last mistress.' Then he picked up the pug and left, delighted to have quizzed me when I was in no position to object.

'I hope the fellow is not a Captain Sharp,' Glandower said. 'My friends will not thank me for bringing him down on their heads if it proves to be the case. Ah, well, he won't skin *me* of much. You can't get blood from a stone.'

We entered the hotel, had wine and the Maid of Honour cheesecakes, which are a necessary treat for all visitors, by legend having been invented by the ladies in waiting to George II when he was Prince of Wales. I was then at liberty to express myself sated and fatigued, and was taken back to the Clarendon.

Edmund, Maisie and Mitzi awaited me in our hired chamber. 'Have you had a terribly dull afternoon, Aunt?' I asked.

'Not so bad as yourself, having to put up with that grinner,' she replied.

'He didn't do much grinning. Did Edmund tell you it is set for tonight?'

'I told her,' he said. 'I am going to the lobby now to see if he left off the address he promised.'

He was soon back, holding a folded sheet of paper in his fingers. 'A Mr Aberdeen at Reddish's Hotel is to be our host. I was hoping the letter would read Downing Street. I was also hoping for a two-handed game. I hope this is not going to be a complete waste of time. What did you make of his attitude this afternoon, Lizzie?'

'Nothing. I know he is short of funds, and wants money for a particular reason.'

'What reason?' Maisie asked instantly, with the utmost suspicion in her green eyes.

'To get married. He is looking for work. I cannot imagine why he doesn't just tell Uncle.'

'He's bamming you,' was Aunt's reply. There was no point trying to convince her otherwise. Her dislike of Glandower was too deep-rooted.

'Let's go,' Edmund suggested, scooping a wriggling Mitzi into his arms.

'Did you get to the bank?' I asked him.

He patted his pocket and nodded. We returned to Belgrave Square and another meal of underdone beef, roasted this time, and enhanced with a few vegetables in honor of my aunt and myself. Edmund left us early, stating his intention of looking over the place before joining the game. I queried his meaning.

'I'll make some discreet inquiries in the tap-room about this Mr Aberdeen before I get involved in any deep gambling. I wish we were going to Downing Street. I'm afraid the grinner won't carry the necklace on him. I was hoping he would put it up for collateral.'

'Are you sure you can *win*?' Maisie asked.

'If the game is straight, I am not worried. If the fellow is a Greek, I shall recall an urgent appointment and leave, before I am thoroughly fleeced. I won't have any trouble recognizing a shaved card at least.'

'We'll wait up for you,' I said.

'Don't. God knows how late I will be out.'

'I forgot it is a hotel you are going to.' Hotels, of course, were his most favored spot for encountering stray females.

He leveled a dark eye at me and shook his head. 'I limit myself to one dissipation a night.'

'What do you mean?' Maisie asked.

'He means he won't drink too much, Aunt.'

'You'll need a clear head,' she said, satisfied with this explanation.

Edmund forgot to draw out his watch before he hastened out of the room, but he did take the precaution of checking the head-and-shoulders clock on the mantel piece, and said it was five minutes slow.

'There is a new thing called a calendar, Edmund. Some people go by the day, instead of the minute,' I mentioned.

'Go to bed,' was his answer.

CHAPTER 14

My aunt and I passed a pleasant evening reading the city newspapers. I remembered Edmund's suggestion that we remain a few days after he got back my necklace. I could see there were many avenues of enjoyment open to visitors, and was not reluctant to indulge in them. At about ten-thirty, Aunt decided to retire. I said I would wait up a little longer. Once alone, I found myself thinking of Glandower, and feeling once more a sympathy for him in his plight. He spoke so hotly and so admiringly of his Miss Millington of the Titian curls, it was difficult to believe he had embarked on a life of crime when he hoped to win her. Surely this was not the act of a young man genuinely in love. Marriage to the right girl would be the very thing for him. It would give him something to live and work for, and, I hoped, cure him of his pernicious gambling habit too. Weston would certainly welcome him at Rusholme. I had very nearly decided to go to Glandower after the affair of the necklace was settled and talk him around to righteousness. In order to straighten out his life, it would also be necessary to talk Edmund out of going to Bow Street. He would never do it without consulting me, as he had more than once mentioned the desirability of keeping the thing mum for Weston Braden's sake.

The head-and-shoulders clock on the mantelpiece wheezed eleven times, telling me it was time to give up my vigil and go to bed. As I arose to shake out my skirt, there was a sound at the front door. Within seconds, Edmund stepped into the saloon, his shoulders drooping. His languid gait made it unnecessary for me to ask how the card game had gone.

'Did he fleece you completely?' I asked fearfully.

'Nope, Aberdeen did. A wily little Scots fellow.'

'A Greek?'

'If he had the cards fuzzed, I couldn't detect it. I think he might have had a few aces up his sleeve, but was so adroit I couldn't catch him at it. I didn't figure it was worth a duel to find out if he was cheating. He didn't quite bankrupt me. I left early.'

'Was Glandower there?'

'Yes, he lost too. We left early together. I have been at Downing Street with him the past half hour. He doesn't seem such a bad fellow really. You don't suppose we could be wrong about him?'

'Maybe Greenie did it all by himself. No, he couldn't have though. It was Glandower who took the necklace to that Mr Anthony fellow.'

'No, it was only someone who bears the same general description as Glandower. We don't actually *know* it was he.'

He took up the carafe of wine and two glasses, poured out some claret, then sat beside me on the sofa. 'You have been holding out on me, Lizzie. You didn't tell me about you and Cummings. Why not?'

'What?' I asked. 'What was there to tell?'

'When you mentioned his desire to marry, you forgot to say it is *you* he hopes to wed.'

'You have got this story dreadfully mixed up.'

'I think not. It has been a wish of Weston's for some time that you two make a match of it.'

'I never heard of such a thing! Why, I hardly *know* the boy.'

'He speaks highly of *you*.'

'It is a Miss Millington he wants to marry. She has Titian curls and a pretty nose, but unfortunately no money. That is the only item she has in common with me.'

'He didn't mention any Miss Millington. He said his uncle would like him to offer for you. I wonder if that is why the poor boy is so bedeviled?'

'Of course it is! Oh, why did he not tell me so? I could have eased his mind in a minute. I could have told him I had no intention of marrying him, and then he could tell Weston, and have a clean slate. That is why he won't go home, why he thinks Uncle would not welcome him and his bride. He is very foolish.'

'He's still wet behind the ears.'

'I am going to tell him what you said about Weston wanting to adopt him. I know Uncle would be happy to see him settle down, and it *would* settle him, if he had a wife.'

'It would certainly help. Your uncle now believes you are

to marry me in any case, so he can hardly push for you to marry Glandower.'

At this point, we stopped talking and exchanged a guilty look. 'How does it come we are worrying about him, when he stole your necklace?' Edmund asked. 'What we ought to be discussing is how we are to get it back. I begin to think the boy has conned us very thoroughly.'

'How do we prove it?' I asked, setting my chin in my hands to aid concentration.

'He's offered the necklace to Mr Anthony, and is afraid to complete the deal, as we have been prating to him of Bow Street. I wonder if we couldn't go back to that shop, and hint to the dealer. . . .' He came to a stop. 'No, he would not arrange a private transaction for us. That cuts out *his* profit.'

'You could offer him a finder's fee – some small per cent or bonus, if he would send Baron Czarnkow to you. Glandower will be happy to unload the necklace privately, I fancy. I sort of hate to do it to him. . . .'

'It can all be kept within the family circle. We'll give him a good bear-garden jaw, scare the living Hades out of him. The important thing is to get the matter settled up quickly. I can't stay away from home forever.'

I saw the London holiday slipping away from me. 'Yes,' I agreed quietly.

We sat in silence for a moment, sipping our wine. 'Cummings didn't notice your engagement ring?' he asked suddenly, looking at my left hand.

'No, but I cannot get it off. I'll try soap and water tonight.'

He nodded, displaying no particular interest. 'Hungry?' he asked.

'No, are you?'

'No. We might as well turn in. We can't do any more tonight. I'll go back to the jeweler tomorrow and see if he is willing to send Baron Czarnkow to me. Glandower has no reason to be familiar with this address. I'll have the Baron come here. What name shall I use this time?'

'You might as well be Sir Edmund Blount. He will know it before long, but at the moment, the name means nothing to him.'

'That's true. I wish I could rid myself of this pity for the demmed jackanapes,' he said, arising.

We extinguished the saloon lamps and went to the hallway, still lit. 'The butler will take care of locking up,' he told me. 'Do you want to come to the jeweler's shop with me tomorrow?' he asked, as we mounted the stairs.

'Yes. Edmund – what if Glandower doesn't go along with this plan? I mean, what if he is not interested in selling the necklace privately?'

He hunched his shoulders. 'We shall see.'

'You *do* believe Glandower is Baron Czarnkow, don't you?'

'He probably is. I was just pointing out the possibility we have erred on that point, as we erred on so many others along the way.'

'*I* never thought Weston Braden was guilty, not for a moment.'

'*Somebody* is guilty, and by God somebody is going to pay for the trouble we have been to.'

'We cannot remain on indefinitely spending your money in this fruitless way.'

'Looks as though we'll just have to go to Cummings and lay our cards on the table. I wouldn't be surprised if he'd be as relieved as can be to spill the whole story.'

'I hope he doesn't break down and cry. I hate to see a grown man cry.'

'He's hardly more than a boy. Younger than Willie.'

'I cannot get over Uncle Weston thinking I would marry him.'

As we had reached my door, we stopped.

'It certainly set me back on my heels to hear it. Good thing you weren't there, as you hate to see a grown man cry.' He tapped my chin twice with his finger.

'It would disturb you that much to see me abandon my principle of misogamy, would it?' I asked.

'Absolutely! We're in this principle together, till death us do part. What God has created asunder, let no man join together. Aren't we lucky we found each other? I don't think you appreciate me. Plenty of gents in my position would be forming honorable intentions by now.' With a disparaging smile, he lounged off down the hall, cleaving to his principles with an unflattering tenacity.

I entered my room and looked at my watch, for no particular reason but that I saw Edmund do it so often. It was eleven-thirty-two.

CHAPTER 15

*I*t's time we put that leg of yours back to work, Maisie,' Sir Edmund said as we sat in the morning over breakfast. 'Come with us.' We had been discussing his lack of success the night before, and the new plan devised.

'It's a decent day. I'll be happy to tag along,' she agreed, 'I won't tackle any long-distance walking, but I can limp to the carriage at least.'

Once we reached the shops, Edmund went alone to speak to the jeweler, while I remained behind with my aunt. He was gone for about ten minutes. When he returned, he was smiling. A smile was attractive to him; I cannot imagine why he used one so seldom.

'Cummings hadn't been back to the shop, but the fellow has his address. Not his Downing Street one, but a hotel, where Cummings must have made some arrangement to pick up messages. Mr Anthony agreed to send a note with my message. If the baron is interested in a private sale, he will be in touch with me. I expect to see him today or tomorrow.'

'How much is it going to cost you?' was my first concern.

'Plenty,' he replied, his smile vanishing.

'Add another fifty guineas to our bill,' I advised my aunt.

'Twenty-five,' Blount corrected.

'A mere bagatelle. We'll have you paid off in no time. Ten years at the outside.'

'It's not funny,' Maisie said, frowning. 'How are we to pay all our bills?'

'It has been understood from the outset I am at fault in the matter, and am to stand buff,' Edmund said, disliking to discuss it, to judge by his repressive expression.

'Mercy, I didn't mean our bills to *you*!' she exclaimed. *You* are the least of our worries. It is the mortgage I spoke of. But Weston will likely take the necklace after all, once we get it back. It was only the botched thing Bartlett made that he disliked. Will thirty-five hundred cover our expenses, Lizzie?'

It was my turn for a damping frown. 'Yes, we will be on easy street,' I lied glibly. We would be out of the woods, no more.

Edmund looked out the window, pretending to be deaf, like a proper gentleman. When we stopped talking, he turned back to us but changed the subject. 'Let us take your aunt for a spin in the park,' he suggested. 'We won't see Glandower at Belgrave Square for hours, if he comes today at all.'

'Yes, she is overdue for some amusement, poor dear.'

'Don't start pitying me,' she scolded. 'We never have any entertainment at home, Lizzie, and didn't expect any on this trip either.'

I glared at her for revealing our dull schedule, but she was impervious to such hints, and went on to outline to our host the usual manner in which we spent our days – tending the garden, the house, taking an occasional sprint into town or to a neighbor's house for cards in the evening.

'It sounds cozy,' he told her, when she had finished complaining. 'Very much the way I go on myself.'

We drove up Bond Street, thence to the park. 'Where would you like to go next?' he asked.

'Let us go home,' I answered. 'You are spoiling us. This pampered aunt of mine will be expecting a Season in London, giving her such a taste of the high life.'

'Maybe we had better get home,' he agreed immediately. 'We wouldn't want to miss him.' He pulled the check string and directed the groom to go straight home, where we sat an hour in the saloon waiting for the knocker to sound. It did not. We then had lunch, and waited for another two hours, during which time Edmund's carpet bore observable traces of a path from his stalking back and forth in front of the window. It is fortunate just looking at a watch and clock doesn't harm them, or he would have required two replacements.

'It's not sure he'll come today at all,' Maisie pointed out.

'He may not come *ever*,' I added.

'He'll come,' Blount asserted firmly.

Before many more pounces back and forth in front of the window, Edmund darted out of his worn path. 'A carriage has stopped – a man is alighting. He's coming!'

By the time we had elbowed Edmund aside to see for

ourselves this interesting sight, the man had proceeded up the walk and was soon hammering on the knocker. I felt a sudden, strong desire to remove myself from the room. I would rather have taken a beating than be present at the scene of Glandower's imminent disgrace. I was too late. He was even then being shown into the hallway, handing his hat, gloves and cane to the butler. He was at the archway to the saloon, bowing and smiling, but soon widening his eyes in astonishment. So were we all. It was not Glandower Cummings at all, but a quite different tall, fair-haired, handsome young man.

'Colonel Fortescue!' I exclaimed, heartily relieved it was only our old traveling acquaintance, who had somehow or other found out my address.

'Mr Aberdeen!' Edmund exclaimed, blinking.

'Baron Czarnkow,' the butler announced, looking at us all as if we were candidates for Bedlam.

The gentleman – I was at a loss now to know what name to call him – turned on his heel and made a bolt for the door, leaving behind his hat, gloves and cane in his rush to escape. Edmund hollered to the butler to stop him, then took to his heels to assist his servant. Before I had recovered my wits sufficiently to have made any sense of the appearance or do a thing to help, Edmund was back, holding the man by the collar till only his toes danced along the carpet, with his two arms paddling futilely in the air.

An oath I was surprised Edmund even knew came out of his lips. He was frowning furiously, trying to make sense of this unexpected appearance. 'Did I hear you call this creature Colonel Fortescue?' he demanded of me.

'Yes, this is Colonel Fortescue – the gentleman I told you about who had his watch stolen at Devizes. Put him down, Edmund, for goodness' sake. There is obviously some dreadful mistake. Colonel, you must forgive. . . .'

'Baron Czarnkow is the name he gave me,' the butler inserted, measuring a fierce glare on our caller, daring him to contradict it.

I went on staring too. If this was Baron Czarnkow, the man who offered my necklace to the jeweler. . . . The truth floated within my grasp, but I was prevented from latching on to it by Edmund.

'Last night he called himself Mr Aberdeen, and used a Scottish brogue. What's your *real* name, sir? Or do you possess one?'

'My friend, Baron Czarnkow sent me—' he started to say, the strain of inventing a new story showing on his face, which was turning an alarming shade of red.

'Edmund,' I implored, 'loosen your hold a little. He's croaking!'

The man was dropped to the floor, with his left arm wrenched tightly behind his back by Blount, who was enjoying the altercation immensely. He looked the way he looks when a raw piece of meat is dangled before his eyes.

'Cut line,' Edmund ordered, giving the arm an extra twist that caused our caller to grunt in pain. 'I *should* have recognized you for a conman when I met you last night. You dealt yourself a suspicious number of aces. Glandower Cummings tells me you regularly enjoy this streak of luck.' This bleater has conned your cousin, Lizzie,' he added, turning to address me over my shoulder. 'They were close

friends. He learned from Cummings in some way that you
were going to Rusholme with that necklace, and met you
en route, to relieve you of it. He was at the inn at Devizes,
I believe?'

'Yes. That is, Colonel Fortescue. . . .' I stumbled to a
stop. 'But his watch! He surely didn't steal his own watch?'

'Steal it? He probably never owned one. He let on it was
stolen, to ensure no suspicion fell on himself. The victim is
always the last to be considered in the light of wrongdoer.'

The man had been making some sounds of protestation.
'I know nothing of this,' he shouted earnestly. His memory
was prodded by another twist of the arm. 'My watch *was*
stolen. I know nothing about the necklace, I tell you.'

'Search him, Ford,' Edmund commanded the butler.
The servant came forward warily and started going
through the man's pockets. The necklace was inside his
inner breast pocket, the second one searched. It was loose,
not wrapped in anything. Ford lifted it out, dangled it
before us.

'My necklace!' I screeched, rushing forward to claim it. I
looked at it in the light from the window, confirming that
it was indeed my own, and not, somehow, another
forgery.

'That settles it,' Edmund said with satisfaction. 'I'll drag
this vermin down to Bow Street. Better come with me,
Ford. He's weasel enough to slip away on me. I'll need you
ladies to press charges.'

'Miss Braden,' Fortescue began, in a beseeching,
outraged, and withal, cowardly fashion, 'tell this gentleman. . . .'

'Handle him with care, Edmund,' I said, in a tone of heavy sarcasm. 'The colonel has a wound stolen in the Peninsula that bothers him, when necessary.'

Maisie had jumped to her feet like everyone else when the man first entered. She had said nothing, being as confused as myself. When she did speak, she only added to the mystery. 'What about Greenie, the little valet who sold the copied necklace at Winchester? That was not Colonel Fortescue. He was Cummings's man.'

'I *told* you I had nothing to do with it,' Fortescue said at once, jumping on this possible bit of uncertainty.

'You had plenty to do with it!' Edmund assured him, with no lessening of his conviction. 'I don't know what Greenie or the copy have to do with it. Nothing, probably, but this is the fellow who nabbed the diamonds. He fits Anthony's description perfectly. He had himself announced as Baron Czarnkow; he carried the loot on him. What do we need, a signed confession? We'll stop at Downing Street along the way, and see what Cummings can tell us about the wretch.'

'He's not at home,' Fortescue told him. 'His uncle arrived in town. They went out for lunch. I was there before I came here, and they were just leaving.'

'Lies won't save you,' Edmund told him. 'I'll drop this fellow at Bow Street first, *then* go to Downing Street and pick up Cummings.'

I was still concerned for Glandower, wondering if he were involved in the plot in some manner. Greenie's unexplained behavior looked like it. 'Let us discuss it a little first, Edmund,' I said, trying to convey by my tone the wish for a private chat, before he went bounding to the Law.

I believe he was beginning to entertain a doubt similar to my own. 'Lock him in the study, Ford, and stand outside the door with a pistol. We want to talk.'

He went with Ford to incarcerate the crook, and to find a gun, then returned, wiping his hands and smiling. 'So there is your gallant Colonel Fortescue, Lizzie,' he told me, his smile triumphant.

'I want to speak to you before you drag him off. What if Cummings is mixed up in it with him? He might have been, for all we know. He did introduce you to the man last night, and we know Greenie is implicated.'

'Greenie's being involved doesn't mean Cummings is,' he replied. This sounded more hopeful than reasonable to me.

'I want to talk to Glandower before we do anything rash. I have got my necklace back, and that is the main thing.'

'If Glandower Cummings had anything to do with it, he ought to be behind bars, the grinner!' Maisie told us, an angry light in her eyes. She would have second thoughts later, however, after her primeval blood lust had quietened down.

'It won't do any harm to talk to him,' Edmund agreed. 'I'll send a footboy around to Downing Street with an urgent message.'

'Don't mention his friend Aberdeen, or he won't come,' Maisie advised him, shaking her red head in astonishment at our concern for a grinner.

'I'll set a guard on the window of the study as well, just to be sure the colonel don't bolt on us,' Edmund said, as he strode quickly to a desk to dash off the note to Cummings. It was dispatched immediately.

I was surprised when Cummings came escorted by Uncle Weston. Fortescue had one truthful speech in him. He had been to Downing Street, and the gentlemen had gone to luncheon, but had returned and came at once to us.

Glandower was forgivably confused to learn that Mr Haskins was also Sir Edmund Blount, my fiancé, as Weston introduced him. It took several moments to go back to the beginning of our trip and explain all our doings over the past several days.

'Why on earth did you not *tell* me the necklace had been stolen?' Uncle asked.

'Why did you not tell *me* any of it?' Glandower asked, his head turning from one of us to the other, as the story unfolded in three jumbled parts.

'It was Edmund's idea. He's a genius,' I answered, dumping the explanations in his lap.

'Finally admitting it, are you?' he asked.

Maisie, still eager to drag Cummings into the thick of the evil, demanded an explanation for his valet's doings.

'I can explain that,' Cummings answered easily. 'Uncle gave the necklace to his aunt.'

'We know how he came by it. Why did he sell it in Winchester?' Edmund asked.

'He took it to give his girlfriend, but the two of them had a ripping fight, and have broken up. She gave it back. He was short of blunt and pawned it. Did it on our way from Fareham to London. He often pawns things at Reuben's place. Some of my mama's gimcrack old costume jewelry and bits of furnishings from her home – stuff that is not wanted at Rusholme. I have to change teams at Winchester, and my valet has struck up an arrangement with Reubens, as his place is handy to the inn.'

'I saw the man with my own eyes at Devizes,' Maisie said in a darkly accusing way. 'What was he doing at Devizes, eh?'

'His home, and his girl, are in Bath,' Cummings said. 'After his fight with her, he wrote me and I wrote back I would meet him at Winchester, to save him the extra fare down to Fareham. The stage stops at Devizes en route from Bath to Winchester. He must have gone to the inn for an ale or something. Lots of people take advantage of the stop. He had already pawned the necklace when I met him at Winchester. We set out immediately for London. It all fits.'

'You never mean that nice Aberdeen lad you had home with you is the criminal you're speaking of?' Weston asked.

'He did *seem* a nice gentlemanly fellow,' Glandower said, with an apologetic look toward us victims. 'I took him home with me last time I went, for a visit. We were to stay a week, but when Aberdeen heard some friends were going to London, he expressed the desire to leave earlier. It happened the very day Mr Braden received your letter telling him you would bring the necklace, Lizzie, but I never made any connection between the two things. How should I? I had no idea he was a thief I thought he made his living at gambling. He is very lucky at cards,' he added inno- cently. Risking a look to Edmund, I saw him roll up his eyes in dismay at the boy's naïveté.

'So he rushed off to Devizes to meet you,' Edmund said, directing his words to myself, but for the edification of us all. 'It was the logical place for you to stop for a change of team – just one stage from Westgate. Had no opportunity occurred there, he would have trotted after you till he found, or made, the chance to lift your necklace.'

'He was very particular, too, to discover my name, and where I was from, to be positive he had the right victim fingered. Like a ninnyhammer, I told him even my desti-nation,' I admitted. 'He is extremely dexterous. I still don't know when he got into my reticule to steal the diamonds.'

'He diverted your attention a dozen times by different ruses,' Maisie reminded me. 'Maybe he did it while you were destroying my bonnet by removing the feathers and burning them.'

'Then he pretended his own watch had been stolen, so no one would think of him as the thief,' Edmund added. 'He has more than his share of gall, to give the devil his due.'

'I wish he might have selected someone other than my valet as his scapegoat,' Glandower commented.

'I expect he wanted someone highly visible – someone with a physical peculiarity I mean, that everyone would remember having seen at the scene. He was likely seen talking to the valet, as they knew each other from their association with Glandower, and it was easy to believe his watch might have been taken during their conversation,' Edmund hypothesized.

'I believe you have your match in ingenuity,' I told him.

Again Uncle Weston demanded why we had not told him the truth, why we had gone to such extraordinary rounds as having a bad imitation made up.

Edmund, I learned, was a more accomplished liar than I had imagined. Without blinking, he answered, 'The police suggested it. We went straight off to a constable, of course. It was his suggestion we not broadcast the theft. He felt it would increase our chance of getting it back if we kept it close. He suggested we continue on our way to you, Mr Braden, as he thought the thief might try to sell it to you. He was aware of your reputation as a connoisseur of antique things, and thought the thief might also be, but hoped he would not be aware you were so intimately acquainted with that one specific piece.'

'I daresay my reputation is growing,' Weston said, willing to swallow this interpretation as it puffed him off a little.

'At the time, we thought the theft was done by some come-by-chance pickpocket. Fortescue, of course, *did* know of your familiarity with the piece, and did not try to sell it to you,' Edmund added in a sincere way.

'You might have slipped me word on the sly, Lizzie,' Weston said a moment later. 'You knew my discretion could be counted on, I hope.'

'I wanted to,' I said, searching my mind for some reason why I had not succumbed to this harmless desire.

'*I* talked her out of it,' Edmund threw in hastily.

'I still cannot understand why you came to *me*, Sir Edmund,' Glandower said, frowning with the chore of trying to make sense of our tale. 'Came as Mr Haskins, I mean.'

I sincerely hoped Edmund's ingenuity held up, for mine was exhausted. 'By that time I had a line on Czarnkow,' Edmund answered reasonably. 'The jeweler mentioned he was a friend of yours.' He paused just a second, to see if this passed muster.

'I *did* go to a few shops with him one day he was hawking his diamond studs, but I don't think I ever went to Mr Anthony's place. I shouldn't be surprised if those diamond studs were stolen as well,' he added, with a shocked face. Really the boy was dangerously innocent, and here we had taken him for a villain. 'It seems those jewelers are all as close as inkleweavers, know what is afoot with their customers.'

'Very likely,' Edmund agreed, concealing his relief very effectively. 'Lizzie then thought you might inadvertently have given this Fortescue fellow some intimation of her traveling with the diamonds, so we went to see what we could learn from you.'

'You should have asked me outright,' Glandower said. I felt it a just accusation, and waited to hear why we had not.

'Bow Street insisted we keep the whole thing mum,' Edmund told him. 'As it turns out, they were correct. I left word with Mr Anthony, who passed it along to Fortescue-Czarnkow, and here we are!'

'I suggest we take the poltroon on down to Bow Street immediately,' Uncle Weston suggested.

It was hard to credit we had scraped through the meeting without offending either Uncle or his stepson. But they were unaware of our high suspicion of them, were not looking for it, and so missed it. With the passage of time and deeper thinking, they would doubtlessly concur we had acted like Johnnie Trots, but at least they would not know why.

We went out into the hallway to see Ford standing at attention at the study door, with a pistol in his fingers.

'Is all quiet within?' Edmund asked him. He nodded smugly. 'Go get a length of rope. We'll bind him up tight. We don't want to lose him after the trouble we've had tracking him down.'

'Would it not be better to have the Runners come here for him?' Weston inquired, with an old man's caution.

The younger gentlemen did not mean to give over their fun so soon. They agreed they were more than capable of delivering a mawworm to custody. Ford came with the rope, Edmund unlocked the door, while Glandower stood with the pistol raised, ready – indeed, eager to judge by his face – to shoot. The door opened noiselessly. A gush of wind blew out on us. The room was perfectly empty of human life. The open window told the tale of Fortescue's escape.

I wouldn't even know how to spell the words that were uttered. Edmund I was coming to know for a prime blasphemer, but to hear Cummings curse like an Irish chairman was a shock. They pelted into the room, stuck their heads out the window, with myself following hot on their heels. There beneath the window lay a prostrate servant, with a welt on his temple. A poker lay at his side, the poker from the study grate.

We ran out of the house, around to the window to revive the servant. Edmund took into his head to give chase to the culprit, but it was too late. He had got clean away. The servant told us the man had raised the window to ask him a question. At a carefully arranged moment, Fortescue had whacked him on the head with the poker, knocked him unconscious, clambered out the window, and got away, without making a suspicious sound.

We returned to the study to see to closing the windows, and for a look around for clues. A pot of ink had been poured all over the desk, to drip onto a fine carpet. It appeared a senseless act of vandalism at first, till Edmund took a closer look.

'My gold inkpot! The son-of-a. . . .' He was looking around the room, and soon noticing other missing objects. Besides the gold inkpot from the days of Queen Anne, a cherished family heirloom, Fortescue had got away with other bibelots. Edmund mentioned a silver letter opener, a faience snuffbox and a broken, gold watch-chain, snaffled from a drawer.

I have never seen Edmund so angry, except perhaps when I made him empty his pockets for me at the inn at Devizes. 'This does it!' he bellowed, his face assuming a liverish hue. 'I'll catch that creeping reptile if I have to tear London apart brick by brick.'

Without another word, he bolted out of the house. Glandower followed fast behind him. I *think* he was smiling. 'An exciting day,' Weston said, mildly dismayed. 'How's about a cup of tea, Lizzie? It will settle our nerves.'

CHAPTER 16

*T*he tea, I am bound to say, proved totally ineffective as a calmer of my nerves, though it settled Maisie and Weston down.

'What made you decide to come up to London, Weston?' she asked.

'The fact of the matter is, I had a falling out with young Cummings last time he was home. My own fault. I blame myself entirely. I have long been urging him to marry Lizzie. An ideal match in my view, but he was not agreeable to it. No reflection on yourself, Lizzie. He had some other girl in his eye all the while, as it turns out. When you arrived with your young man, I saw my plan was gone all awry. I wanted to make it up with him, so I came to London to see him. He had not told me about Miss Millington, you must know, or I would not have pushed Lizzie forward. My greatest concern was for him to settle down, and if he has found someone he likes, I am sure it will do admirably. They are to stay at Rusholme, of course,' he added happily.

'Do you know the girl? Have you met her?' Maisie asked, always interested in romantical doings, especially in the family.

'Certainly I know her. She lives not five miles from us. Glandower met her at a local assembly. A good family, not terribly well-to-grass, but more than respectable. The father is a solicitor, and the mother somewhat better. *Her* family is related to the Crossleys.' I had never heard the name of Crossley, but it was obviously meant to confirm the girl's gentility.

'Have you spoken to him about changing his name – the adoption, I mean?'

'Not yet. There is no rush on that score.'

'When is the wedding to be?' I asked.

'He hasn't asked her yet. Still, he is in no doubt that she will have him. It will do the boy a world of good to get out of the city. Such acquaintances as this Fortescue would be the undoing of him. Now that it is out the scoundrel is a thief, it is no harm to say ten guineas were missing from a metal chest I keep in my room. I thought Glandower might have borrowed it and forgotten to tell me. Not that he has ever done so in the past, mind you, but he will sometimes ask for a little more than his allowance, and he did not on this visit.' 'A little more' sounded a strange description of five thousand pounds. So did the word 'borrow' seem inaccurate for stealing. It was a gauge of his affection for Glandower, that he should be so generous in his descriptions.

'Glandower will be a help to you at home,' I mentioned.

'He claims to know nothing of farming, but I will be

happy to teach him. He is sharp as a tack, will pick it up in no time. It is almost like having a son of my own. I think he will agree to adoption. He is in a mood to agree to anything, since I have agreed to his offering for Miss Millington.'

'That will be wonderful for you both. All three – I must not omit Miss Millington,' I complimented, while my mind tore through the streets of London in pursuit of Colonel Fortescue. I wondered what his true name was.

'Well, you have got the necklace back, Lizzie. Shall we have a look at it?' he asked soon.

It was held tightly in my hand. I did not lose track of it this time. I gave it over reluctantly. Anything that causes so much trouble is valued. I was extremely loath to sell it, but our financial straits were as tight as ever.

He smiled fondly at the antique. 'The price I mentioned . . .' he began tentatively.

'*My* price is not a sou less than four thousand, Uncle,' I cautioned.

'I was about to say three thousand is all I can see my way clear to paying at the present time. With the expense of the wedding, you know. The children will want a wedding trip, and a new mistress in the house will want to make some improvements. She will have modern ideas about fixing things up.'

'*Modern* ideas at Rusholme?' Maisie asked, staring.

'In the kitchen and pantry, I mean. Naturally, she will not be hacking down the ancient timbers, or tearing out my fine old glass windows, but if she wants to make some improvements in the kitchen, she may do so with my blessing. Cook rants at me twice a week about conditions there. It looks fine to *me*, but the women like to be up-to-date in their housekeeping.'

Of more concern to me was the reduced price for my heirloom. I reached out and took it back pretty quickly. 'I am not interested in selling at that price,' I told him.

He let it go from his fingers, his eyes following it covetously. 'Maybe in a year or two . . .' he said. 'Expenses will be lower without the London apartment to keep up.'

The relieved look on his face referred to gambling debts rather than the upkeep of a small apartment, but he wished to keep Glandower's sins beneath the cover. The boy was only foolishly immature, not bad.

'Let us wait and see,' I answered, slipping the necklace into my skirt pocket.

I became so restless, sitting and sipping tea when every fiber longed to be out with the men, that I arose and said I would take Mitzi for a walk. I got no farther than the corner when I saw Edmund's carriage wheeling down the street at a dangerously fast clip. Glandower was still with him. They spotted me from the window, and had the carriage checked. I grabbed Mitzi up and hopped in.

'Did you catch him?' I asked.

'Yes, the damned fool went to his hotel to pack up his bags and bolt out of town,' Edmund replied. 'We knew where he stayed of course – Reddish's. I also got my inkpot and snuffbox. The bastard had already sold my letter opener, or stuck it into someone's back. If we read a report of such a murder weapon, we'll have him hanging from a gibbet. He is in custody now. The Runners feel this will solve a number of mysterious thefts that have plagued the city recently.'

'Did you find out who he is?' was my next question.

'He's got so many aliases he keeps a list, along with what accent accompanies each character. I doubt if he remembers his real name himself. He is often a Scots squire. Douglas is the first name on his list, if that means anything. They want you to go down to Bow Street and file a complaint, Lizzie. Demmed unpleasant for you, but it must be done.'

'Unpleasant? I look forward to it with the greatest relish!'

'What, ratting on the gallant Colonel Fortescue?' he roasted joyously, luxuriating in reminding me how I had misread the man's character. His face wore a look of fiendish glee.

As we were within a block of his home, we had time for little conversation. Glandower tendered an apology for having brought this pest down on our heads.

'That's all right,' Edmund said magnanimously. 'If it hadn't been for Lizzie losing her diamonds, we two would never have met, you know.'

'Yes, we would,' I reminded him. 'You knocked my carriage off the road before the theft.'

'That is true, but there is no saying things would have worked out so well for us if you had not accused me of stealing the diamonds myself.'

'I didn't realize your friendship was so new,' Glandower said. 'The way you carry on – I mean, you act like very *old* friends.'

'*I* am over thirty, and Liz admits to twenty-five, so can likely give me a few years,' Edmund answered playfully. 'We are very old friends.'

'We were acquaintances before the trip,' I said, lying again.

'Yes, we met over a year ago, when I bought some cattle from Westgate,' Edmund added. 'Nothing like a good business deal to cement a relationship. But it was only after the accident we became close friends.'

'It was an accident that made Miss Millington and myself realize how well we suited, too,' Glandower answered. His head was so full of his Miss Millington he only half heeded our conversation. He went on to speak of spilling wine on her gown at an assembly, and her ripping up at him, which in some mysterious manner caused her eyes to sparkle, and her hair to glow, and all sort of other incredible change occur in her appearance. He was in a sort of dream state, enthralled at how well his life was sorting itself out. Much better than my own. It would be back to Westgate for me, still in debt to my ears.

Maisie and Weston had to hear the tale of the chase, capture and eventual incarceration of the Colonel-Baron. Then it was Edmund's turn to hear of Glandower's bride's plans for the kitchens of Rusholme. Odd she had told Glandower so much, with never a *positive* offer from him. He even knew what brand of range she intended to install, and what sort of new chinaware she favored.

As it was getting late, Weston and his stepson remained to dinner, it being settled they would come to us in the morning to accompany us to Bow Street.

'After which we'll get straight on to Rusholme,' Weston said, with a blissful sigh.

Cummings's sigh was possibly even more than blissful. Ecstatic is not too highly colored a description of the look on his face.

'Plan an early wedding, do you?' Edmund asked.

'As early as Meg – Miss Millington – will countenance,' he answered. 'When will you and Lizzie tie the knot?'

'I shall give you the same answer,' Edmund replied. 'As soon as Lizzie will countenance.'

Their questioning gaze turned to me, awaiting my decision. 'We have not discussed the date yet,' I said.

'Don't wait too long,' Weston urged. 'You're getting on, my girl.' He seemed to have forgotten he had not married himself till he was an old man. 'Sir Edmund is no longer a stripling either, if you won't take my saying so amiss.'

'Better late than never,' Edmund smiled lazily.

The company did not remain long after dinner. I felt happy to see them leave together, laughing and talking in perfect harmony, with the future shining brightly before them.

'I hope you're satisfied,' Maisie grumped. 'You've done Jeremy out of his inheritance, and lost out on the sale of that dashed old necklace into the bargain. I for one am coming to hate the sight of it.'

'I feel just the opposite. I am more fond of it,' I answered.

'Let's have a look at the alleged necklace,' Edmund said, holding out his hand.

I took it from my pocket and gave it to him. He observed

it silently. 'Put it on,' he ordered.

In the excitement of our afternoon and evening, we had not dressed for dinner. The jewel did not show to good advantage on a muslin gown, cut too high at the neck to do it justice. I went to the mirror, folded back my collar, and modeled the piece for them. The flickering lamplight made my image dark. The queen was, back, her red crown sitting proudly. It quite took me back to that evening at Westgate, when I had seen her in the dining room mirror. It had been a strangely upsetting evening. It was Maisie's telling me about her crush on Beattie that had lent it an emotional tinge. That, and her wondering if I ever planned to wed. As I stood, looking and remembering, Edmund's head loomed up behind me in the mirror.

'Aren't you going to let us have a look?' he asked. We stood, looking at each other in the mirror.

'I've seen it a million times. I'm for bed,' Maisie said, still in her disgruntled mood. 'Goodnight to both of you. Don't be late, Lizzie. We'll be leaving tomorrow, I suppose?' she asked Blount.

He did not answer immediately. 'We'll see. Goodnight, Maisie.'

She limped from the room, grumbling to herself. 'What's got into her?' he asked.

'The new closeness between Cummings and Weston. Not a hope for Jeremy now.'

'It doesn't bother you?'

'I came to terms with it long ago.'

He nodded, hardly paying attention to my answer, to

judge by the faraway look in his eyes. 'Are you in a hurry to get home?' he asked.

'I should be getting back. You have mentioned more than once you must too.'

I was not actually in so great a hurry I would not have objected to a few days gallivanting in the city. 'I have an excellent steward,' he said. 'You, I know, are not so fortunate in that respect.'

'No, I certainly am not.'

'I was thinking – tell me if you dislike it. I could stop off a day or two at Westgate and look the place over for you. Perhaps recommend some improvements to your operation. I don't mean to boast, but my farm is considered one of the more outstanding in the neighborhood. I told your uncle I would see to hiring a new steward for you. I would be perfectly willing to do it.'

'That is an untoward imposition on your time and goodwill,' I replied, disappointed at his reason for visiting us.

'Yes, but imposing on my time and humor have not prevented you from taking advantage of me in the past,' he pointed out.

'Kind of you to offer, but it is not necessary. We'll manage.'

'As you like,' he said at once, his face assuming a stiff-as-starch look. 'There is nothing more to be said then, is there?' was his next indifferent statement, with a quick look towards the head-and-shoulders clock. 'Eleven o'clock already. I expect you are eager to get to bed.'

'I was about to suggest it,' I was obliged to reply.

'I shall say good evening to you now. As we are leaving

tomorrow, I plan to have a night on the town. I hope you will sleep well.'

He walked swiftly from the room, mounted the stairs two or three at a time in his haste to get into proper clothing for seducing members of the muslin company. That was his reason for going out. I knew it, and believe he told me his plans on purpose to upset me.

I waited till I heard his bedroom door slam before leaving the saloon and going to my own room. It was no queen who glared back at me from my mirror, but a thoroughly annoyed spinster. I wrenched so hard at my necklace I bruised my neck.

CHAPTER 17

It was difficult to judge by Blount's glowering face across from us at the breakfast table whether his outing had been successful or not. It could have been simple fatigue that lent that sullen line to his mouth and kindling spark to his eyes, or it could have been frustration.

'I hope you ladies enjoyed a good night's rest,' he said, making an effort at civility for my aunt's sake. Had we been alone, I don't believe he would have bothered to even nod.

'I slept like a top,' I assured him.

'I didn't. It's hard to sleep in a strange bed,' Maisie said. 'I'll be happy to get home. Have you decided when we are to leave, Edmund?'

'As soon as we have returned from Bow Street.'

'Good. God only knows what Berrigan has destroyed in our absence. At least there's nothing left for him to cut down. You must replace him as soon as we are home, Lizzie.'

This speech set Edmund to scowling harder than ever. I

interpreted his accusing stare as disapproval of my not accepting his offer to perform this task for us. 'Try if you can find someone who realizes infected cattle are not to be sold,' was his cheerful comment.

'For God's sake eat your raw meat, before you bite our heads off,' I snipped back.

'I do not feel like eating today. I shall have a cup of coffee.'

While we, Maisie and I, picked at our breakfast and Edmund took an occasional sip of his drink, there was a knock at the door. I expected it would be Weston and Glandower. I could not imagine what was afoot when Jeremy was shown in.

'What on earth brings you here?' I demanded.

'I learned from Aunt Maisie where you were staying,' he answered, with a challenging look towards Edmund.

'This is my brother,' I told our host. He nodded, with very little interest.

'I wrote him of our adventure,' Maisie explained. 'Gracious, I didn't expect you to come all the way to London, Jeremy. That was not necessary.'

'I am surprised you did bother to come,' I added, as I was cross with Edmund, and felt like taking it out on someone.

'When my sister is run off the road and injured by a "gentleman," when her diamond necklace mysteriously disappears while in his company, and most particularly when I hear she is *masquerading* as his fiancée, though he has no notion of marrying her, I feel it is time I come,' was his haughty reply, accompanied by a hard stare at

Edmund, who looked back with his jaw dropped open.

'Well, if this doesn't beat all the rest!' Blount exclaimed, his voice high with incredulity.

'I would like to have a word with you in private, sir,' Jeremy continued, acting the noble protector. I wanted to throw my plate of bacon in his face.

'Don't be such a peagoose,' Maisie told him. 'Sir Edmund has been very helpful to us.'

'Why are you staying at this house, a bachelor's establishment?' Jeremy demanded, fixing me with a suspicious eye.

'Because, thanks to your incompetent management of Westgate, we cannot afford an hotel!'

While we shouted at each other, Edmund slammed down his cup and rose slowly up from the table, leveling a baleful look at my brother. I envisaged a duel. Something in the way they glared at each other put the image in my head.

'Come into my study,' Edmund said in a cold voice. It was not an invitation, but a command.

Fearful of what might pass, I hopped up and followed them, despite Maisie's hands grabbing at my skirt to hold me back. 'Jeremy, don't be a fool!' I said as we went. 'Edmund has been extremely kind, very helpful to us. It is his doing that we got my necklace back.'

'It was *his* doing that you lost it,' my foolish brother countered.

'If you're looking for a fight, boy, you've got it,' Edmund told him, closing the door rather hard behind him. 'This is the second intimation I have had from the Braden family that I am a thief. One cannot call out a *lady*; a gentleman is not so protected.'

'Apologize *at once*, Jeremy!' I ordered.

'What about the necklace?' he asked, looking with uncertainty from me to Edmund, but mostly at the murderous expression in Blount's eyes.

'I have got it back. Sir Edmund had nothing to do with its disappearance.'

'What of the sham engagement?' he persisted mulishly, but in a less arrogant manner.

'That is irrelevant – a ruse we dreamed up between us to take Edmund to Rusholme. No one will hear of it.'

'You shouldn't have been selling the necklace in any case, Lizzie,' he said, deciding I was a more vulnerable opponent.

Edmund was already simmering; this question took him beyond the point of restraining his tongue. 'As questions are the order of the day, Mr Braden, let me pose you a few. How does it come you place the burden of running a derelict old heap of a farm on two ladies? Your mismanagement has done the dairy business more harm than the plague. I personally suffered the loss of two dozen prime milchers, and know others who were damned near wiped out. Your sister was kind enough to undertake selling her inheritance to pull you out of the suds, and *you* have the insufferable gall to upbraid her for it. My great crime in the affair was to be sideswiped by your sister's carriage. As a consequence, I have been accused of common thievery, involved in brawls, arrested for assault, bitten by a dog, missed my brother's wedding, spent several days and a considerable amount of money trying to find the damned necklace. I have been reduced to gambling with criminals, having my own property stolen and must now go to Bow Street to try if I can to clear the matter up. If you have something to say of your sister's spending a few nights under my roof, with her aunt as chaperone, pray say it now, and have done. You may be sure you will be called to good account for it. If *you* have no more sense than to accuse your own sister of improper conduct, you are not worth killing, but by God it will give me satisfaction to knock your teeth down your throat.'

He looked ready to do it. His fingers were already curled into fists. Jeremy swallowed a couple of times and began backtracking. 'What was I to think when Maisie told me about the accident and Lizzie having her diamonds stolen?'

'If you had any common decency, you would think how you might help her!' Edmund answered swiftly, angrily.

'That is exactly what I *am* thinking!'

'It is of no help coming here and creating a scene!' I told him.

'I don't mean that! I am going to sell Westgate, Lizzie. My mind is made up. *I* don't want it. I will be taking a post at Oxford when I graduate, and mean to remain there permanently. The farm is nothing but a nuisance to me. I'll sell it. With the mortgage paid off, there will still be enough to buy a small cottage near the university, or I can live there.'

'What about Maisie and me?' I asked, nonplussed at this turn, though selfishness from my younger brother was no new thing.

'You two women can't run the farm,' he pointed out. 'You already proved that.'

'Let him sell it,' Edmund advised. 'The best news I have heard all year. Let someone who knows what he is about take it over. A mismanaged estate is the worst nuisance imaginable.'

'But where will Maisie and I go?'

'Accept Beattie's offer,' Jeremy suggested. 'Or if you don't like him, marry someone else.'

I was not about to reveal the lack of suitors to my host. 'We'll discuss this later,' I said quickly. 'You might have told us your plans, Jeremy. It is of some interest to us, you know, to learn we are about to lose our home.'

'Uncle Weston would be happy to have you at Rusholme,' was his next suggestion. He had not yet heard of Glandower's plan to deliver a new mistress to that establishment, nor would he have seen any difficulty in three mistresses, if it came to that.

I accepted this home, in theory, to terminate the highly unpleasant conversation. 'Uncle Weston is in town,' I mentioned. 'He will be here shortly, to go with us to Bow Street. We can talk later.'

'I still have a great deal to say to you,' Edmund warned him. 'You also have something to say to me. I have not heard any apology.'

My brother looked more confused than apologetic when Blount stalked from the room; leaving us alone.

I had not the least desire to come to cuffs with Jeremy at this time. I wanted more than five minutes to ring a peal over him, and Weston would be here within that space of time. 'I hope you're satisfied!' was all I said, before bolting out the door after Edmund. He did not bother to follow. Already his eyes had strayed to some bookshelves along the wall.

When I reached the dining room, Edmund was laughing with Maisie, restored to good humor by some magical means. Maisie inquired after my brother. 'He's in the study, and I hope he stays there. He is selling the house on us, Aunt.'

'I know. Edmund just told me.'

'I am surprised it has put you in such good humor.'

'It is the best thing could happen to us,' she replied. 'Edmund suggested old Beattie might be glad to get it back. It used to be part of his estate, you know, and he could well afford to buy it if he wanted.'

'He never mentioned wanting it,' I reminded her.

'Not in words, but you must remember we have more than once wondered if his offering for you was not because he thought the house was in your name. You said so yourself.'

'I don't remember anything of the sort! Of course he knows it is in Jeremy's name.'

'Edmund thinks the best thing is to go home and not let Beattie know we are eager to sell,' she outlined. 'He has an excellent plan, as he always has,' she added, with an approving smile at her new protege. 'He says—'

The knocker sounded, preventing my hearing his excellent plan. It was Uncle and his stepson. I got my wrap and bonnet, Edmund his hat and gloves, and we two were off to Bow Street to make our report. Maisie was busy ordering the servants to prepare delicacies to tempt Jeremy's jaded palate.

The visit to Bow Street was not in the least unpleasant. I thoroughly enjoyed laying charges against Fortescue. With some persuasion, Edmund arranged it that we not have to remain for the trial, as my property had been returned. We left off signed statements. They had plenty of other witnesses ready and willing to testify that Mr Douglas-Aberdeen-Fortescue-Czarnkow was assured of a long spell of free lodging.

Uncle Weston and Cummings left at once to terminate the lease on the latter's apartment and get him permanently returned to Rusholme. They parted with all manner of cheerful promises to call on us, along with requests for us to come and see them on our wedding visits. We agreed amiably to this absurdity, then went to Edmund's waiting carriage.

A festival mood descended upon us as a result of seeing our wrongdoer safely locked up. Edmund was sure the fellow would pick a lock or break a window and be back on the streets in no time, filling his pockets with stolen goods, but I did not fear that lightning would strike twice. It would not be *me* he preyed on next time. The rest of the world must fend for itself.

'What was the plan Maisie spoke of, about selling Westgate to Beattie I mean? I cannot think how he will offer if we are to conceal from him the news we want to sell.'

'Trust me. I'm a genius, remember?'

'Don't *you* be making plans behind my back too. What

a *stupid* thing for Jeremy to do, not telling us he means to sell. I want to apologize for his lack of manners.'

'I believe it runs in the family. Was I too hard on the cawker?'

'Not half so hard as I mean to be, when we get back.'

'His instincts were correct at least, to defend your reputation. You don't suppose he will force me to have you? Marry you, I mean.'

'I never heard of an unlicked cub forcing a full-grown grizzly bear to do anything. Tell me the great plan Maisie spoke of.'

'I thought I might visit with you a few days at Westgate, letting word seep out I am interested in buying the place. When Beattie hears it, he will, we hope, take the idea that if it is to be sold, it would better be reannexed to Eastgate. He will make you a counter offer, and Jeremy will accept it. *Voilà!*' he said, splaying his hands in triumph.

'*Voilà* what? Who is to say he will be so compliant as to make this offer? I never heard such rubbish in my life. We must put it up for sale in the regular way. I see absolutely no merit in your scheme beyond its novelty.'

'That's odd. Maisie saw the merit of it at once.'

'I am not so sharp as Maisie. Tell me.'

'The point is, it provides me an excellent excuse to visit you, as my first pretext of hiring you a steward was rejected out of hand, and with very poor grace too, I might add.'

'I thought you were eager to get home.'

'I am, but not alone,' he said, taking my left hand in his. My heart speeded up. 'Marriage and other disasters have the reputation of occurring in threes. We have Willie and his bride, Glandower and his, now I fear my number has come up.' His other arm slid around my waist.

'You had no luck with your prowling last night, in other words, and are feeling amorous.'

'You understand me uncomfortably well. No luck. My heart was not in it. I think you know where it was.'

'Those are dangerous words, sir. When a man starts letting on he has a heart, his first object is to lose it to some poor lady.'

'They don't come much poorer than you,' he was uncavalier enough to remind me.

'I meant poor in the "poor Willie" sense.'

'Ah, Willie! I find myself envying him of late. I have lost not only my heart, but my head as well.'

'Next thing to go will be your freedom. What of your misogamy?'

'It got smashed to bits, along with my carriage wheel. I expect it is even now lying in a ditch outside of Devizes, gasping its last gasp. Poor devil.'

'I would make a perfectly wretched wife, Edmund. I am a nagging, foul-tempered harpy, who would keep you under cat's paw.'

'That is exactly the sort of lady I require. A watering pot would not suit me. I recognized you for an archshrew when you advised me to find a strong-willed woman, provide her with a club, and marry her. I considered it just one step shy of a proposal when you said it. Shall we go shopping for a club now?'

'Let us go home instead. I expect you are eager to get

fighting with Jeremy, and I feel an urge to kick my mutt.'

'I am not feeling at all bellicose at the moment,' he insisted, his arms tightening around my waist. 'I will just remind you, however, you cannot get my ring off, and your alternatives are to either lay legal claim to it, or have the finger removed by surgery. It is entirely up to you.'

'I think with a little butter—'

'Think again!' he said, and attacked me, very angrily, in the carriage, in broad daylight. I was subjected to a fairly brutal embrace which I enjoyed thoroughly, though it left my composure, to say nothing of my toilette, in a shambles.

'Try to remember I am not one of your pickups from a public inn!' I gasped, when he released me.

'No, you are much more accomplished. Just wait till I get you that whip to defend yourself.'

'*Club*, Edmund, and don't think I won't use it.'

'Don't think you won't have to!'

Our voices had risen somewhat above a normal conversational tone. We both realized it at once, and laughed. 'We're off to a fine start, aren't we?' I asked.

'Nope, we haven't started yet. High time we did.' He reached for his watch with an impatient gesture.

I sighed to consider the large job I was taking on, keeping pace with him.

Also by Joan Smith
and soon to be published:
FRIENDS AND LOVERS

THEIR MEETINGS HAD BECOME
PITCHED BATTLES

Wendy's brother-in-law, Lord Menrod, was an arrogant, high-handed, albeit dashing, tyrant who was no more fit to be the guardian of children than a dancing bear. So Wendy thought. The children in question were orphans. Nephew and niece to both Wendy and Menrod. But Lord Menrod was wealthy and Wendy was not. Even so, she decided to fight for custody with every means at her disposal.

Oh, how she hated him.

Feelings ran high on both sides. And then something strange happened. Wendy stopped hating her enemy. . . .